Tk

Rough Waters Series
Book One

Danielle Stewart

Copyright Page

<u>Synopsis</u>

Autumn Chase is painfully aware grief is a beast that won't be chased off before it's ready to leave. When an icy road and a dark night leave her a young widow, she's forced to trade in her perfectly planned future for the unknown. Like a child hiding from a monster, she pulls her covers up over her head with the intention of sheltering herself forever. But once an unexpected stranger shows up on her doorstep, Autumn has to choose between being alone or connecting with someone who is hurting   as   badly   as   she   is.

Noah Key, an emergency room doctor, has solemnly informed countless families that their loved one could not be saved. However, when his own wife dies suddenly there are no words to bring him comfort. His in-laws want him to fall to pieces to confirm his love for his late wife. His colleagues want him to take time off to grieve. The only thing Noah wants is to work enough hours in the day to forget his wife is gone. He's written himself a prescription for a cocktail of distraction and exhaustion in order to trick his brain into thinking his life isn't in shambles.

When the world keeps moving on without them, Noah and Autumn will need to decide if they'll survive the storm or allow themselves to be swept away by it.

<u>Chapter One</u>

Snow makes the world mysteriously quiet. It snuffs out the background noise and constant bustle. It slows everything down. But the sound of twisting metal and the screech of wet tires clawing for traction can break the silence wide open. A quiet night can be shocked back to life with the wrong swerve of a steering wheel or the careless lack of attention to a sudden curve in the road.

Whatever the cause, the two cars that collided on the dark country road had just disrupted any peaceful silence the blanket of fresh snow had created. Rolling hubcaps and shards of glass spider-webbed with blood flew from the impact as if fleeing the scene, searching for safety. As the crumpled metal and broken plastic settled, the world ground to a halt. The chilling silence of a wintry night snuck back around them, and only the hissing of leaking fluids remained.

A red mid-sized car lay across the dual yellow lines separating the road like a hurdle that would have to be jumped if someone wanted to get by. Its lights faded as the car's life bled away. Inside a low hiss of static came crackling through the radio.

This isn't at all like the movies. That's all Autumn remembered thinking as the impact sucked the air from her lungs. It wasn't slow or dramatic with time to watch your life flash before your eyes. She hadn't had the chance to remember her favorite Christmas memories or the smell of her husband's cologne. It happened in a blink, a breath, a flash. The ambulance wasn't there in minutes, and no good Samaritans were rushing to her side. This was reality. A quiet road and a late night crash.

When her body and mind finally found each other and melded together, she forced her eyes open. She hardly recognized the interior of her car. She was no longer facing forward but couldn't quite understand how her twisted body had settled.

She wondered what to do in a moment like this. Should she scream? Try to move? Or just close her eyes and wait for help? And then, like so many times in her life, she asked a very familiar question—what would Charlie do?

Her husband of seven years, Charlie, was her guiding North Star. With his instinctive tactical and strategic problem-solving skills, he could maneuver any situation, social or business, with a calculated and deliberate plan. In her youth, Autumn had been a free spirit, motivated by what felt right rather than what looked right on paper. After years of her instincts guiding her down the wrong path, Autumn finally began enlisting the direction of her husband. He always knew what to do.

She conjured up the thoughts of his past advice and searched her memory for something that would carry her through the pain and fear that was beginning to overcome her. There was a moment in time she felt afraid, and Charlie used his logic to calm her down.

One summer night at a carnival Charlie had convinced her to take a ride on the Ferris wheel. From the ground Autumn remembered thinking the ride looked exciting and romantic. But as they mounted their swinging seat, a sudden wave of terror seized her.

Charlie, recognizing the fear in her hazel eyes, sprang into action. In his deep and charming voice he whispered quietly, "It only lasts a few minutes, honey. Just close your eyes. You can do anything for a few minutes. Remember, Autumn, mind over matter." He held her hands in his and squeezed them. Just like that the fear began to subside and she managed not to scream "Stop the ride!" to the kid flipping the switches at the bottom. When the ride was finished, they laughed. Secretly, she said a thankful prayer for putting Charlie in her life. He was everything she was not.

Now, feeling tangled within a web made up of confusion and car upholstery, she repeated that phrase in her mind. "I can do anything for a few minutes. Oh Charlie, I hope you're right." As she thought of her husband again she was suddenly stung by a terrifying epiphany. She remembered she wasn't driving the car when the accident occurred. Regaining focus, she realized she'd been the passenger. The driver had been Charlie, and he was completely silent. She knew him well enough to know that if he had the ability to speak right now he'd be calling her name to make sure she was all right.

Thoughts of her own safety dissolved, quickly replaced by fear for her husband's well-being. Now the thought of staying put and waiting calmly for help was no longer an option. She had to get to him no matter what condition she was in. Mind over matter.

She hesitantly moved her legs, wiggling them slightly to see whether or not she could pull herself out. With a few abrupt and labored motions she managed to free herself. She'd crawl over the mangled front seat and help Charlie.

With hands cut by shards of metal or glass and thin lines of blood running down her arms, she sensed her right arm was broken. In spite of the pressure within her stomach ratcheting up to a burning pain, she muscled her way to a sitting position. She was horrified to find the hood and engine of her car torn completely away. She prayed she'd lean over the front seat and find her husband, possibly unconscious, but alive. Instead she was faced with a crushed steering wheel and a gaping hole from the broken driver's side window. She feared he had been ejected and could now be somewhere in the cold snow, alone and hurt.

Autumn was certain she couldn't muster the strength to crawl out of the car and search for him. She knew the tingling in her legs and the blood pouring from her elbow would soon render her too weak to move.

Whispering Charlie's name, she felt the ache in her stomach grow. She slumped forward and breathed in deeply, hoping to rally enough energy to climb out to help her husband. A cold, snow-filled wind blew in through the broken window, carrying with it the howl of a man's voice. It didn't sound like Charlie, but maybe, in pain, the shriek was all he could muster.

Pulling herself over the bent steering wheel, she dragged her already tender stomach across the remaining glass, sticking up like ragged teeth from the smashed driver's side window. Tumbling in a graceless heap to the frozen earth, she jerked her injured body away from the car, yelling her husband's name out into the night.

Autumn rested her tired and swollen face in cold snow. Reaching her breaking point, she couldn't crawl, yell, or blink anymore. She was empty, completely spent. With her last fuzzy, fleeting thought she prayed Charlie would hold her one more time.

Chapter Two

Noah was certain he was dead. He'd seen every moment of the accident as if it was playing out on a screen in front of him rather than actually happening to him. He felt the force of the impact on his shoulder and legs. The rush of air from his airbag and the pressure on his face was like nothing he had ever experienced before. A running loop of his own voice kept echoing in his head saying, *this is how it all ends.*

When the dust from his airbag settled, Noah jerked forward. He pushed the extra material away from his face and reached to his right. "Ray," he called out. His wife, Rayanne, had been sitting in the passenger seat, and he knew she would be terrified.

He knew he was hurt. He knew the car had been torn nearly in two, but nothing could prepare him for the image of his wife burned into his retina. It was clear the moment he saw her; it would be etched in his mind until the day he died.

He clamped his eyes shut at the sight of his wife. Her limbs were twisted and broken. Her neck was completely wrong, bent awkwardly to one side. Her beautiful blue eyes were white. They'd rolled upward as if looking at the car roof no longer there. The roof had been peeled back in the impact like the lid on a sardine can. Noah, a doctor of eleven years, knew in an instant his Rayanne was dead.

Instinctively, Noah reached out to her and placed his fingers on her neck, searching for a pulse he was certain he wouldn't find. There was no longer any life inside her. His methodical, medical mind sprang into action, spinning through his knowledge, searching for something that could help. Even though he could see her neck was broken, and she'd most likely died on impact, it was almost impossible to accept that there was nothing he could do to bring her back.

A brief, unfamiliar wave of panic washed over Noah. He let out a blood-curdling scream that carried on a winter gust out into the dark night. He jiggled the driver's side handle of the SUV, pushing his tender shoulder against it, but to no avail.

He heard an unexpected response, a woman's voice laced with desperation and horror. He couldn't make out what she yelled, but he connected deeply with the primal core of her voice. It rose from deep inside her shattered heart, filled with pain and confusion, and right now that was the language he was speaking.

He tried forcing his mind to recall other moments in time. He drove himself to remember every family he'd consoled when he broke the bad news to them that their loved one hadn't survived. Noah tried to shove his torment out of the vehicle and as far away from his mind as possible.

Another scream came from outside the SUV. Though it was hard to admit, Noah knew there was a mission greater than just surviving. There was someone else injured, possibly dying, screaming into the night, and as a doctor he had taken an oath to help.

Noah lifted himself forward. He was resigned to the fact that his door wouldn't open. He tried the button to lower the window but it wouldn't work either. The front windshield was smashed out but the engine was exposed and smoking. He didn't think he could safely maneuver over it. The only feasible alternative would be to crawl over Rayanne and out through the shattered passenger's side window.

Like so many times before, Noah chanted a familiar phrase, "Just finish it." It was the mantra that carried him through difficult and nerve-wracking moments, like his proposal to Rayanne, and now it would push his body through this. With this simple phrase he was able to turn his emotions off, letting his intelligence take over. It was the only way out of the car, so he'd just have to do it.

Lifting his upper body toward his wife, he chanted again, "Just finish it." As his face passed hers, the fabric of his pants caught on a tangled piece of metal, and his aching body collapsed atop his wife, knocking the cell phone she'd been holding to the SUV floor. He hesitated for a moment, wondering if he should grab his cell and call for help, letting his weight linger on top of her. He smelled the sweetness of her skin and the familiar freshness of her pin-straight golden hair. Noah fought the weakness he battled almost every difficult moment of his life. He had a desire to bury his face in the nape of his wife's broken neck and join her in death. If he could, he'd stay like this forever, but his brain knew better. He couldn't allow himself to dwell on the fact that this would be the last time. There were other things to be done tonight.

As he did in so many instances before, Noah crammed down his emotions and shoved his body forward. That's what a man does. That's how a doctor gets through the days where nothing makes sense. Careful not to disturb his wife's body, he wriggled out of the SUV.

Standing for a moment, he gathered his strength before looking in awe at the wreckage around him. Before he could begin his search for the source of the heartbreaking screams, he heard the sirens and saw the blue flashing lights of the cavalry.

Chapter Three

Autumn's arms itched as her wounds began to heal, covered with thick scratchy scabs. It had been four weeks, one day, and six hours since her husband had been killed in the accident. She wondered when that ticking clock maintaining a morose countdown would finally stop; the thought terrified and exhausted her. She didn't want to keep remembering how long it had been, but she didn't want to lose track either. If she stopped paying attention to that, would it mean she didn't care enough anymore?

She had finally washed the medicinal smell of the hospital out of her hair. She had eaten something more than crackers and had cast Charlie's pajama shirt into the wash. Her husband's smell had worn off and that reality brought her even lower. Whether she liked it or not, life was continuing to crawl forward around her. Every passing minute moved her sixty seconds further from Charlie.

The first two weeks she lay imprisoned in a hospital bed made immobile by tentacle-like IV's and beeping monitors. People, unrecognizable ghosts claiming to be her closest friends and family, drifted in and out of her hospital room. They sobbed, comforted, and said all the wrong things. They reminded her in hollow monotones, and with heartless insensitivity, how "everything happens for a reason."

These apparitions whispered promises and offers of *if there is anything you need* and *I'm just a phone call away*. Just three days after her arrival home the phone calls suddenly ceased, and the casseroles stopped arriving. These close people scattered like dying, wind-blown leaves, settling back into their own self-centered routines.

Autumn couldn't blame them. They were a mix of co-workers, neighbors, and second cousins. They'd done their part, now able to wash their hands of the suffocating sadness enveloping her with a clear conscience.

The only person diligent and selfless enough to continue his visits was Charlie's father, Mike. He had lost his wife more than a decade earlier to breast cancer and had just recently won a personal battle with melanoma. The cancer ravishing his face, the surgery, and the extended treatment he'd undergone seemed to age him well beyond his sixty-one years. He'd already been through so much. But like clockwork, he showed up.

Mike had visited every day in the hospital. He wasn't crying or offering meaningless words of hollow comfort. He just sat, kind blue eyes under furrowed overgrown dark brows, looking earnestly over his daughter-in-law. He hadn't asked what happened, he hadn't begged for the details, and he hadn't cursed God for such blatant injustice. He'd just visited—sitting quietly, and occasionally humming to himself. Autumn didn't know the tune or even care much for the roughness in the old man's throat, but it was better, immeasurably better, than anything anyone else had offered. The man had lost his son, and yet he found a way to be strong for her.

Autumn's own parents were over a thousand miles away. They had traveled to be with her in the hospital, standing as rigid as statues at Charlie's funeral. They shook people's hands, ate the food, and boarded their plane for home. It wasn't any more or less than Autumn had expected from them; it was in fact a perfect representation of who they were. They were physically present, but could be as invisible as a fading mist on a hot summer morning, burned away by the intense heat of emotion. Comforting made them uncomfortable. Sadness to them was similar to the common cold, if you exposed yourself to it long enough you were bound to catch it. The best prevention was to stay clear of it.

Mike, however, was just present enough. He was gone when she wanted him gone and seemed to arrive whenever she needed him. He hadn't pushed her to get out of bed or shampoo her dirty unwashed hair. He hadn't told her to brush her teeth, or wear something other than Charlie's plaid button-down pajama shirt. He just existed at the borders of her reality and allowed her to exist. He'd always been a wonderful father-in-law but this was a gift, something she could never repay him for.

She recognized features on Mike's face that had clearly been passed down to Charlie. She had never noticed the grey flecks in the blue of his irises that caught the light much like they did in Charlie's eyes. She had overlooked, until now, the uncanny similarity to random features like the shape of their necks and how similar their thumbs were. It seemed ridiculous to miss Charlie's thumbs, but at the sight of Mike's clone-like pair, she felt so weak.

This morning when the doorbell rang, she pulled the covers of the spare bed over her head. She hadn't slept in her own bed since the accident, afraid to deal with the empty spot beside her. She imagined it would be like a rowboat without oars or a candle with no wick, and once she faced it alone, she would slowly forget what it had been like to lie there in his arms. Trying to keep his smells and his presence alive and around her was like trying to hold a puddle of dripping water in her hands. Every passing second, a trickle of Charlie slipped away.

The doorbell rang again. It couldn't be Mike. Normally, he'd have let himself in by now. Ringing the doorbell was his warning shot to let her know he was there. It was someone else, some other bumbling idiot here to say how sorry they were. She felt like asking what the hell they were all so sorry about. Had they brought the snow that night? And if not, why the hell were they apologizing? Wasn't there anything better to say? Oh yes, the ever-popular *God works in mysterious ways*. That was one of her new favorites.

She let the doorbell ring three more times, each irritating tone stealing more breath from her lungs. There is no one, she thought, who could be so cruel and so invasive as to terrorize and practically stalk her this way. She told herself that, for all she cared, this heartless person could ring the doorbell until their finger started bleeding. She was staying right there in bed, as usual.

Her routine consisted of staying awake until the sun rose and then submitting to her body's biological need for sleep.

After finally dozing off at sunrise she would awake around nine o'clock in the morning and stay motionless in bed for nearly three hours. She wondered how she didn't go mad or get bored, but boredom never seemed to come. She would will herself out of bed, avoiding every mirror and every clock as if it were the devil reincarnated. Next on the list was eating something, something completely unappetizing to any normal person, like a Danish with olive paste or a cookie dunked in pickle juice. She had never eaten such disgusting combinations before, but something inside of her was broken. Nothing tasted good, but nothing seemed to taste bad either.

After some atrocious combination of food had been eaten at warp speed, the newest addition to her routine would unfold. A shower in water so hot it made her skin red and stole her breath. She would stand beneath it for over an hour, waiting to feel better, or clean, neither of which ever seemed to happen. Inevitably the water would run cold, Mike would show up, and it would be time to give up.

She had begun dressing again in clean clothes and wearing deodorant, something she had truly forgotten existed over the last month. Last week she had dropped her toothbrush in the toilet and had not replaced it, just thrown it away like it was the last one she'd ever use. Her bottle of hair gel was empty, and she decided her curly brown locks were best left untamed. Their wiry rebellion articulated her feelings in a way words could not. People got the point quickly when they saw her hair. Mad woman. Crazy hair was a good way to keep people from talking to you.

When Charlie died in the crash, she'd lost far more than spilled blood and torn flesh. There were large chunks of her life she could never recover, and the sparkle in her eyes was one of them.

She felt she'd shriveled up, like the accident had taken actual inches off of her. Everything and everyone, no matter the size, seemed to tower above her now. Without her husband and their plans for the future together, her existence had become meaningless.

There were now only small victories. Like the fact that whoever was at the door had gone away. She knew by the angle of the sun pouring into the sparsely decorated spare bedroom, as useless as it seemed, it was time to start her day. At least every hour that ticked by brought her closer to being back in this bed to hide.

<u>Chapter Four</u>

Noah wept for the loss of his wife only once. During one of his shifts, in the privacy of the handicapped stall on the first floor of the emergency room, he let salty tears pour from his dark brown eyes. His lashes, turned up to the sky, held onto droplets of tears as if unsure of what to do with them. He hadn't cried in nearly sixteen years and had no intention of making it a habit. He knew this moment called for crying; he knew he deserved one excused breakdown in order to be able to move forward.

The accident had left him bruised and tender, but his injuries were not life-threatening. He was out of the hospital and burying his wife before the week was through. He slipped quietly back into his episodic life, treating endless trauma victims in the emergency room, taking double, and sometimes triple, shifts to avoid dealing with the outside world.

With his parents constantly urging him to take some time for himself, they'd worn out their welcome in his two-bedroom home. He hadn't needed to tell them to leave. They could understand the subtle manner in which Noah spoke without words. Hell, they had taught him that language, being perfectly fluent in it themselves.

Rayanne's family had never cared for Noah. It was unspoken but clear to everyone. In their eyes he was distant and never seemed to understand the importance of family. When he missed the family picnic or showed up late for Christmas Eve dinner, it was like he'd committed some cardinal sin. How dare he not be there to see Rayanne's sticky-faced little cousins unwrap their noisy toys. No one ever asked about the patient he'd saved that night or the family who had their father back from the brink of death because of his long hours of work. They just shot snide remarks and dirty looks his way.

Jack and Donna, Rayanne's parents, were pillars of the small Connecticut community where she'd been raised. They owned a local store and had been everything from babysitters to godparents to almost every child in town. It was a life Noah never envied or understood. It seemed so time consuming to be constantly available to everyone. In his eyes they had no privacy, no vacation, and no life of their own. It wasn't until recently he had realized his career had put him strangely on the same path as his in-laws. He was just as busy and preoccupied, but instead of being available to those who loved him, he was absent when it mattered most.

He was shocked slightly by the anger he saw in his mother-in-law's eyes. It couldn't be labeled fury or malice, but it was there all the same. He interpreted it as bitterness and blame for a life wasted. The responsibility for Rayanne's death was not being cast upon him but rather the responsibility for the troubles of her life. Perhaps an untimely death is more easily accepted if the life before it was fulfilling. But he could tell her parents felt he'd robbed her of that.

He shook the thoughts, too deep and sad, from his mind by splashing cold water across his face. The door to the bathroom creaked open, and he knew his moment of trembling sorrow was over. Straightening his jacket and raising his chin in an act of feigned composure, Noah let out all the breath he had stuffed in his lungs. As if he had not been crying and his wife had not just died, Noah left the bathroom and moved effortlessly back into his day.

"Dr. Key, you have a visitor in the break lounge; do you feel up to company?" a stocky faceless nurse called out to Noah. All the nurses seemed faceless to him. They all wore the same clothes, did the same job, snapped the same gum, and told the same boring stories. One nurse was no different than the next.

"Who is it?" he asked, snapping back at her. He wasn't sure which made him angrier, the empathetic, kid-glove approach every one had taken with him since the accident, or the commonplace inept manner the hospital staff used to relay this information. Noah wanted to say, *mind your business about whether I am up for it, and tell me who is waiting for me and how long they have been there.*

"Donna Ripper," the woman answered, taken back by his tone.

"Great." Noah groaned. "Tell Dr. Lopes not to steal my patients. I will be back in five minutes. He takes every opportunity to take all the good ones." You had to be a doctor to understand who the "good" patients were. The more maimed or mutilated, the bigger the challenge, the better the patient. In the small hospital a doctor slow to the charts could end up doing sutures or enemas for his entire shift.

As Noah walked away he heard something to the effect of "You can take more time if you need to."

Bracing himself for the unknown, Noah scanned methodically through his brain to try and determine why Rayanne's mother would visit him at work. As usual, he had no concept of time, leaving his watch in his locker during his shift. It sat on the same shelf, by his wedding ring, day in and day out. He was more than a creature of habit; there were times he was a slave to it.

Noah pushed open the door to the hospital break room and saw his mother-in-law staring out the wide plate-glass window that faced the parking lot. Noah had always thought of Donna as a beautiful woman, but now her face sagged with sadness. She had clearly missed more than one night of sleep, and her need for coordinating clothes had slipped away. Instead of her normal matching jogging suit or bright floral blouse with crisp linen pants, she wore a sweatshirt with tattered sleeves, and upon further review, Noah realized her shoes didn't match each other.

He felt sorry for the toll his wife's death was taking on Donna. He imagined her world being ripped apart and replaced with some dreadful and insufficient fraud of an existence. Rayanne was her only child and now would never realize her dreams or the unfulfilled dreams of her mother. Donna's one hope at redemption and recapturing lost opportunities had died weeks ago.

"Noah, where have you been?" Donna asked, her voice cracking with trepidation. She swallowed hard to try and hide her obviously shaking body.

"What do you mean Donna?" he asked, knowing perfectly well what the poor woman meant. Her question was laced with anger. *Why haven't you called? Why had you skipped Uncle Manny's sixty-seventh birthday party? Is this what our life will be now, will we lose you too?*

"I haven't heard from you. Nurse Wendy at the front desk said you've been working an unimaginable amount of hours, and you just haven't been yourself. I'm worried about you, Noah." Donna moved toward him but stopped just short of touching him. They had never had that kind of relationship. Rayanne was clearly the bridge that gapped the differences between them, and Noah wasn't sure there was anything left for them now that she was dead.

"I don't even know which one Nurse Wendy is. They all gab too much, and you can't trust what they say. I'm doing okay. I just need some time to get my work straightened out. We're understaffed and this place never sleeps. You know how it is." Noah knew she didn't understand how the hospital worked or how the rush and the pace brought him some kind of perverse comfort. It kept things like his wife's death in perspective. It reminded him that people died every day, and they left many people alive to miss them. He wasn't alone, and he wasn't the worst off of all of them. At least he wasn't saddled with motherless kids. Some poor bastards had no money or nowhere else to go when they lost their loved ones. He had financial security, the strength to stifle his emotions, and a job that took most, if not all, of his attention. Even today he had seen people much worse off than he.

"I went to see Autumn Chase today. I wanted you to go with me, but you didn't answer your phone. I had you paged, but I didn't hear back, so I went without you. I thought you would want to be there, but I just hadn't heard back." Donna rambled and Noah tried to keep pace with her choppy and fumbling words.

"Donna, who is this Autumn? I'm sorry I didn't call you back. Like I said, it's crazy here and—" Noah stopped speaking at the sound of Donna's heavy exhale and the wave of her hand. She clearly didn't care to hear his feeble excuses. She looked as though she were about to yell something to the effect of: Who gives a shit about this dump and these people? I want my daughter back, and if I can't have that, I want everyone in the world to miss her the way I do.

Instead she continued laying trails of words between them, some making sense and others running right into the next.

"Autumn was in the other car that night. She lost her husband, and I went to visit her today. What if she doesn't have anyone; what if she needs a meal or a friend? The woman just lost her husband, and I'm sure she's a wreck." The last sentence was meant to cut at him. As though she were saying falling completely apart was precisely what anyone in his position should be doing.

"How do you know where she lives? I'm sure she has plenty of people in her life to help her, if she needs it." He emphasized the "if" hoping strangely that it cut her equally as deep.

"It was in the paper. Besides the articles about Rayanne, there were ones written about Autumn and Charlie. That was her husband's name, Charlie. I just thought you might want to come and show your support." Obviously nervous, Donna pushed her thumb through a hole in the tattered sleeve of her sweatshirt. Noah thought it such a childish gesture for a woman of her age.

A pang of nervousness suddenly struck him. What if the woman, the person in the other car, had some memory of the accident? What if she recalled his SUV swerving across the

17

yellow lines, ignoring the posted speed limit in spite of the snow? What if the police figured out just what had been going on between him and Rayanne before the crash?

The police report had listed no one at fault. It had been ruled an accident caused by weather conditions. So catastrophic was the wreckage that very little scene investigation could take place. It was labeled a definite tragedy, but not a crime, and Noah wished it to remain that way. But what if for some reason new evidence appeared, and they reopened the case? Shit.

Trying not to sound agitated, Noah asked, "Well what did she say?" His heart skipped a beat, and he pushed aside his longer dark hair that had fallen on his forehead, a motion that was as much a part of him as his limbs. It was a move that he unconsciously did now but had rehearsed as a young man trying to maximize his looks and appeal. It was the movement that had drawn Rayanne to him from across a crowded Christmas party many years ago.

"Nothing. She didn't answer the door. I rang the bell for God knows how long. I was sure she was home. There was a car in the driveway, and there were some lights on. I left her a note. I wonder if she is just so broken up she can't even come to the door."

Noah had the impulse to say, "Yes Donna, I understand; by not falling apart in your arms I am doing a grave injustice to the memory of your daughter." Instead he let kindness win out.

"Well, maybe that's a sign," Noah said, playing into Donna's desire for everything to be directed by some higher power, something he had always brushed off. "Maybe she was out or really doesn't want any company. I know how hard this is. I know that it was so unexpected and just doesn't seem fair. I promise it will get better with time." He brushed his hair back again and wondered if she was experiencing the same disconnect between the verbal conversation and the words clawing at the back of his throat, trying to escape. They were unthinkable and insensitive words he wouldn't voice to his worst enemy but his desire to hurt Donna was growing. He wasn't sure why.

"I just thought it would be good for you to meet her, maybe befriend her, but perhaps you're right. Leave well enough alone."

It was an empty concession, and he knew she knew it. Donna would try again to meet this woman Autumn just as Noah would brush off the idea when it came up. It was like leaving a Band-Aid half on. You knew it wasn't helping, but ripping it off held the promise of pain, so you just leave it hanging there, annoying but familiar.

"I've really got to get back to work. I'll give you a call." Noah smiled, being noncommittal as usual.

"Yeah, I'd like to come by and go through some of Ray's things, maybe this weekend?" Donna sniffled and looked to the ceiling unable to hold back the tears that had gathered at the corners of her eyes and now blazed trails down her hot pink cheeks.

"Um . . ." Noah stumbled. "I hadn't really thought about it. I guess that would be okay; I'll be working most of the weekend, but you can let yourself in and take whatever you want." He had been home no more than one or two hours at a time since the accident. He knew there were dishes with decaying food in the sink, sour milk in the fridge, and plants dying for water.

He had been either on a treadmill at the gym, sleeping in his car in the hospital parking lot, or working. This left no time to surround himself with Rayanne's clothes or books. He had steered clear of her pictures and ignored the answering machine with her angelic voice telling anyone who called that Noah was out on the ark and she was gathering two of every kind of animal. It was a joke she loved to tell and while it didn't make him laugh, the image of her wrinkled nose and squinting eyes as she'd lost her composure trying to record the message always made him smile.

"Okay, but isn't there anything you want for yourself?" Donna asked, posing a blatant test of his love for her daughter. Surely any man who lost his dear wife would have some treasures that he would lay his life on the line to keep safe.

"I'll put a few things away, but for the most part whatever you'd like is fine with me. I know how special some of her things are to you, and they'll be safe at your house." To bring a clear close to the conversation, Noah pulled the door to the break room open, letting the noises of the hospital spill in. Without another word he walked away.

Chapter Five

Autumn flipped through the pages of her old journal and rolled her eyes at how trivial her entries used to be. Today she put pen to paper and began to write again, this time something that felt worth the effort.

2/27

It's amazing how the little things seem to slip away when your life turns upside down. When I read a few pages back in this journal I realized how trivial my worries were. How silly it was to write about when Charlie left his shoes all over the house and how Sherri at work parked in my spot for the hundredth time. Was that really the worst thing in my life before?

There are so many things I haven't done in the two months since Charlie died. I haven't slept in our bed. I haven't watched our television shows we used to never miss, and I haven't driven my car. I've been reduced to being Mike's passenger, and I insist we leave the radio off, not so we can talk but so I don't have to hear a song that stirs memories of my life before the accident. Mike has been going far beyond his father-in-law duties, and I'm grateful for it.

I don't know how he puts up with me, since I can barely put up with myself at this point. My whole existence seems to be bisected by a thick blood-red line. When I talk I seem to preface everything with before Charlie died or after the accident. It's like my life can be folded in half, and everything I've ever known falls on one side or the other.

The insurance money has come in. For some reason I can't bring myself to spend it, as if once I do, it seals Charlie's fate. I'm waiting for someone to wake me up and tell me if I pay them all the money back they will return my husband to me alive. Like it's a ransom I'd gladly pay. Unfortunately, being

21

out of work for the last two months doesn't leave me with much choice. At some point I'll have to cash the check. I'm dwindling our savings account down.

Mike has done everything from paying my bills to making my meals. The first month or so he let me sleep all day and cry all night. He didn't ask any questions or tell me to take a shower. Now either his seemingly endless patience is running short, or he knows it's time to start moving me along. He wakes me at eight thirty every morning and turns the shower on. He brews coffee and puts the morning news up loud enough to echo through the house and rouse the walking dead. Me.

I've decided not to go back to work. I hate those people. Their trivial problems, office antics, the drama, I just refuse to let any of that back into my life. I wasted so many conversations with my husband, complaining about their bullshit. I wasted so much time, worrying about marketing projects and deadlines instead of holding my husband tight and living my life.

There seem to be so many moments with Charlie I regret. I don't regret my time with him, but what I chose to fill the time with. It all seems so senseless. Complaints about my parents, bickering over what color to paint the den, but what I regret the most are moments I spent not speaking with him at all for some long-forgotten reason. What a waste.

Now I just have to figure out how to get through the days without him. I have to decide what to do with the small things that cross my path. Like how Mike brought me a note that was taped on the front door. Someone has been ringing my doorbell lately no matter how many times I make it clear I won't answer it. Now at least I know who it was. The note read: Mrs. Chase please call me day or night when you have time to talk. Thank you, Donna Ripper.

It included her phone number but I don't know anyone by that name, and I don't intend to call some perfect stranger.

Before Charlie died I was a curious person, always looking for an interesting spin or potential adventure. Not anymore.

I never imagined food would lose its taste and colors could actually bleed into each other. I knew Charlie was part of me, but I didn't realize he was all the good parts, all the exciting, sexy, logical parts of me. I've heard people say they felt empty before, and I thought I understood what they meant. I thought they were using a metaphor and that truly feeling empty wasn't possible. Now I know exactly what they meant, the sensation is as tangible a feeling as hunger, exhaustion, or acute pain.

Mike is urging me to go to grief counseling. He says after his wife died the grief group he met with literally saved his life. He says it's awkward at first, but once you get comfortable it really helps. I'd like to believe him, but I can't imagine anything will ever truly help me.

The night of the accident, New Year's Eve, he kissed me at midnight as the ball dropped and then I buried my face in his neck, kissed it softly, and breathed him in. I lingered maybe a moment too long, causing him to ask that familiar question, "What's wrong?" I replied, "Nothing dear," as I often did to that question, but this time, unlike most other times, it was the truth. In that moment, there was nothing wrong with the world. I don't know what kept me nestled there for those few extra moments, but now I wish I had never let go of him.

Autumn closed the cover of her journal and let the tears roll down her face. She found it strange the way crying had now become so irrepressible. Her disobedient tear ducts leaked whenever they saw fit. She remembered a time in her life when she forced tears, fought tears, and even faked tears; any control she wielded over them was now gone.

Wiping her eyes with the spare room's rough blanket stung, but she was happy for the pain. It reminded her that some of her sensations still existed. She was not completely numb after all. She thought of the stories she had heard of people who cut themselves intentionally. The thought never made any sense to her, but now as she sat rubbing her eyes and feeling the prickly pain she began to understand.

Mike knocked on the door, and she gave her usual answering grunt. She heard the shower in the hall bathroom turn on and knew it was time to meet another futile day. At least she'd started journaling again. That was an accomplishment she had to acknowledge.

She stared around the spare room and tried to stop her brain from connecting everything around her to a memory with her husband. The house she and Charlie had bought six years ago was a three-bedroom, two-bath model home on a cul-de-sac. It was the house they had dreamed of. Over the course of their relationship they had shared a third floor apartment on the shifty side of the city and a townhouse they bought after their wedding. Both places served their purposes, but this house instantly became their home.

They'd redecorated, painted, and remodeled the house until there was nothing left to change. The kitchen was as Autumn had always wanted it, and the office was the perfect workspace for a lawyer like Charlie. They had talked about the possibility of children, something they wanted but couldn't commit to. They'd been waiting for the "right" time but that'd never seemed to come. A pending vacation or work promotion had continuously bumped the plans further and further away. Both Autumn and Charlie understood if they brought the topic up and pushed hard enough, the other would agree it was time. But neither seemed passionate enough, and therefore the topic remained a smoldering thought rather than a burning conversation.

That was a hell in her brain she couldn't wander into. The idea of not making time to have children with a perfect man like Charlie was the regret of her life. She couldn't allow it in. Instead she dragged herself through the mourning.

After her shower Autumn dressed in the clothes Mike had laid out over the bathroom sink. She was in awe of his ability to match an outfit perfectly, a skill he had not passed down to his only son. Charlie had never been diagnosed as colorblind, but if you had ever borne witness to his first-choice outfit in the morning, it became clear as day he had a problem.

As she pulled her shirt over her head, she thought of the old rituals she would never experience again. Each morning Autumn would let Charlie pull clothes from the closet and lay them out on the bench in the master bathroom. Then as he showered, steam filling the room and clouding his view, she would switch out the blue tie or yellow dress shirt for something that matched.

That was a game the two played consistently all the years of their relationship. There were days it was unspoken and funny to both of them, and days Autumn wished he would just do it himself. But now, as there was no one left for her to dress, Autumn found the irony in her clothes hanging over the sink. She was the one needing the help.

Almost three months she thought to herself as she moved downstairs toward the smell of toast and the sound of the morning news. What will this look like in five months or a year?

They exchanged their good mornings, and Autumn pulled a stool to the island in the kitchen. Mike was the unwavering and dependable force he had always been, though the shape of his mouth seemed different today. It curled at the edges as if he had something he wanted to say but wasn't ready to test the words on her fragile soul just yet.

"What is it, Mike?" she asked, her mouth half full of toast. She had decided a few weeks earlier that widows didn't need manners. You could be forgiven of almost anything when your heart was so broken.

He was taken back by the question. She hadn't been the first to speak in the morning since the accident. It had normally taken him an hour's worth of mindless small talk to get her alert.

25

"You look like something's on your mind. Is there something you want to say?" She saw the shock in his eyes but had woken up this morning feeling slightly different, not a marked improvement to her well-being, but some small shift inside. Like something had been partially dislodged.

"I was just thinking," Mike croaked, clearly not ready to have this conversation. "I was thinking it might be a good day to go out. We've done some doctor's appointments, we've met with the lawyers, but we haven't really been out. Are you feeling up to a trip?" Mike spoke as tentatively as one might speak to a drowsy baby. He seemed to know the ice he had just ventured onto might not hold his weight very well.

"Sure. I don't want to see anyone, no one we know, but I think it's a good day to go out." She again filled her mouth with toast and watched victory spread over Mike's lined face. She was happy to give him this small win. It meant she needed to actually find some socks that matched and a hat to cover her long brown hair, but it would be a payment toward the debt she'd incurred from all of Mike's help.

Mike turned the radio off, and Autumn dropped into the front seat of his car. It was incredibly comfortable in that senior citizen kind of way. There was nothing flashy or new about the car, but the seat was wide and the material was soft.

Autumn had dressed in thick oversized layers, knowing a February morning in New England could turn fierce without warning.

"Where are we going?" she asked, feeling suddenly like a prisoner. Mike laughed quietly at first, then it grew to a full cackle, rising up from his stomach. A flash of fear shot through Autumn, who tried to read his expression.

"Please don't be mad," he started. "I wasn't expecting you to say yes today, so I have no idea where to go. I just figured once I got driving I'd come up with something." He spoke through his laugh, and Autumn couldn't help but join him. "Any suggestions?" he asked with a playful grin.

"I think the orchard would be nice. I know the trees are bare now, but at least it will be quiet." Autumn hadn't visited the apple orchard in February. She took comfort that nothing about it would be painfully familiar or remind her of Charlie.

As they pulled up to the deserted farm Mike studied Autumn's face, making sure this destination was still acceptable. They left the car, slipped their hands into gloves, and zipped their coats to their chins. Mike waved to the familiar owner, who was repairing the fence that surrounded the front of the orchard.

The limbs of the apple trees were bare and twisted like old arthritic arms pleading to the puffy clouds overhead. Everything was gray; the trees, the sky, even the grass seemed to be a dull, gunmetal gray. Standing among the endless rows gave Autumn a feeling of daunting hopelessness but comforting company. She felt like one of the trees, abandoned not only by their leaves and fruit, but also by their spectators. The seasonal people who came to smell their sweetness and stand in awe of their vast beauty had all moved on to less unsightly things. There was a good chance when the sky returned to blue, the leaves sprouted poetically back, and the luscious apples were ripe and plentiful all these fickle friends would return, but who wanted those kinds of friends anyway?

"I guess I picked a pretty sad place," Autumn sighed, feeling bad for dragging Mike out to a depressing spot.

"It's not so bad. You just have to know where to find the beauty." Mike bent, putting one knee down on the damp soil. He picked up a golden leaf that had mysteriously survived the bitterness of the winter. It was rimmed with specs of ice and stood erect and frozen even as the wind blew at it.

Autumn smiled and thought how hard that leaf would have had to work to retain its color and keep its shape. She hoped she too would survive the harshness of her life.

"I have some news, Autumn. I would love to say it's not terrible, but frankly it is." Mike stopped Autumn and faced her, seeming as though he were afraid to look her in the eyes.

"I'm not in remission anymore. I was so focused on this damn melanoma I let other things slide. It's colon cancer, and it's spreading something fierce," he said matter-of-factly. "They've offered me some experimental treatment, and I said hell yes. I have every intention of kicking this thing's ass. I love you, and I wish I could spend this next year waking you up and taking you to orchards, but I can't. The treatment is in Texas. I fly out tomorrow, but I can't go if I'm not one hundred percent certain that you'll be all right." He stopped his rehearsed speech at the sight of Autumn's hands waving in front of him.

"Mike, I'll be fine. You need to go do whatever it takes to get better. I'm feeling better every day," she lied, forcing herself to smile through her panic. "You have done so much for me over the last two months. I'll be back on my feet in no time. We need to focus on you now. Can I do anything to help?" She put her gloved hand on his shoulder and did her best to seem stable.

"No, there won't be much anyone can do this first week. Alice will be coming with me. I'll call every day and keep you up to date on when you'll be able to come." Autumn smiled at the thought of Alice. She was a lifelong friend of Mike's, and it was clear to everyone she was in love with him. After his wife died they had grown close, but no one was sure what their relationship really was. That was the nice thing about it. It was private. Whatever it was, it was theirs.

"Well, I guess there isn't much else to say. Life isn't very easy, is it?" Autumn was unable to control the tears streaming from her eyes. They had betrayed her again. She felt the wind blow against them, and they seemed to crystallize as they fled down her chin.

Mike grimaced at her solemnly. "I'm going to be fine. I need you to do something for me though. When my wife died I took it pretty hard. I hit the bottle, nearly lost my job, and it took waking up on the front lawn with a huge gash on my forehead to snap me out of it. Alice recommended a grief

28

group that changed my life. I need you to go to one. I won't be able to get better unless I know you're doing what you need to. Can you promise me you'll go?" They had begun walking back to the car, too sad to continue, too scared to face each other.

"I'll go," Autumn sighed. She knew this day would come eventually. She knew there would be a next step in healing, and she assumed it would probably come before she was ready. Everything did these days.

Without Mike flipping on the light and turning on the shower, she was sure her days would never start. They would bleed, morning into noon, noon into night— nothing accomplished, and nothing gained.

After they got back to her house, her nest of solitude and safety, he had given her the address of the grief group, kissed her cheek, and had done his best to mask his fear. Autumn wasn't clear which of their two battles he was more troubled by. He would undergo surgery, treatment, and recovery while she waged war on a far worse disease, chronic grief. She watched his car back cautiously out of her driveway, wondering if it would ever return.

Chapter Six

Donna sat cross-legged at her smartly decorated breakfast nook. She stared unseeingly at the swirls of cream that clouded her now cold coffee. It had been four torturous months since the night her phone rang with the news of her daughter's accident. The loss was a weight heavy enough to hunch her shoulders with sadness. Any previous priorities had vanished, and now she worked only for one thing, the strength to get out of bed each day.

She had spent the last few weeks being rejected and neglected. Her husband had unplugged himself from their relationship and sunk into a silent depression. Her son-in-law, Noah, had cut her out and the only other survivor of the accident, Autumn Chase, had ignored her attempts to connect. Donna had lost her value as a mother, a wife, and a person. The benchmarks by which she had always measured herself had dissolved. Her life had become a car wreck, or at least the carnage of one.

It didn't seem to matter anymore how moist her roasted chicken was or how the stainless steel of the kitchen appliances gleamed. The crispness of her window treatments and the designer tag on her new blouse were irrelevant. The currency by which she once calculated her worth had become obsolete and meaningless.

Many years ago Donna had sacrificed a promising career in business to raise her daughter. She invested time, energy, and love to ensure when Rayanne walked into any room she could hold her head high. She taught her daughter to read and to love. Now as she sat over her matching embroidered placemats she realized it was all for naught. Every tear she had cried, every curfew she had enforced, every Band-Aid she had applied, added up to nothing.

Her doctor had prescribed antidepressants Donna had avoided taking, convincing herself they would do no good.

The medicine she needed was the touch of her husband's hand or the sound of her son-in-law's voice. However, as the likelihood of those things happening faded, the little peach pill became more appealing. In fact she was terrified to admit that perhaps a cocktail and a handful of the blue pills had become a very real possibility.

The phone rang twice before Donna realized it. As she became less invested in her past life, the people who were once a part of it had begun to fall off. Her friends had stopped calling, their invitations ceasing abruptly.

"Is this Donna Ripper?" The unfamiliar voice had Donna thinking an evil telemarketer had stirred her from her troubled musing. She hissed a breathy acknowledgment to the caller that they had indeed reached the right person on their list. It wasn't until she heard the quiver in the caller's voice that she realized this was no solicitor.

"My name is Autumn Chase. You left a few notes on my door. I hope this isn't too forward, but, do I know you?" The silence on the phone was thick enough to cut with a scalpel. After a long moment Donna found the words to reply.

"You don't know me, not directly. I'm very sorry for all the notes, but I wanted to speak with you. My daughter died in a car accident." Donna held her breath, closed her eyes and continued. That very true statement still felt impossibly hard to say out loud, but she pressed on. "The same accident you lost your husband in, and I guess I was just looking to—" And in that moment she realized she had no idea what she was looking for. She'd spent weeks trying to reach out to this woman, and now that they were connected she was drawing a blank.

"I'm sorry. I can't help you." The quivering voice replied to Donna's stumbling pause. "Don't call me again. Don't leave me any more notes. I just want to be left alone."

When Donna heard the click of the disconnection, she was certain it was the sound of her fragile heart breaking. The weakness in her knees overcame her, and she leaned hard against the kitchen wall. She let herself slide ungracefully to the floor. The sobs that escaped her now were those of true pain. They were not the controlled tears she had let trickle out on the day of her daughter's funeral, still hoping to appear as a strong, willowy matron even in mourning. These were the cries of a completely broken woman drowning in loneliness.

The time that passed, as she lay melting on the floor, was immeasurable. She heard the ticking of her embellished cranberry-colored clock, but it did nothing beyond occasionally reminding her to breathe.

When a key slid into the door she felt her pain turn to panic. It was frightening to think people who held keys to her home were not close enough to her heart now to let them see her deteriorate like this. How had she become so cut off from everyone?

Noah pushed the kitchen door open and crossed the breezeway before Donna could compose herself. She had managed to rise onto her hands and knees, but the moisture around her eyes and nose had not been wiped away.

"Jesus, Donna." Noah hustled down to her level, slipping easily into his medical persona. His cool hand found its way to her pulse, and he counted out the beats against the hands of his watch.

"I'm fine," she said an octave too high to be convincing. She pulled her wrist away and wiped fiercely at her face. "I was just . . ." She dug deep for a lie that wouldn't come. "I was losing my mind here on the kitchen floor. I don't know how long I've been here, and I don't know how to feel any better," she admitted.

"Donna, come on. Get up. Maybe it's your blood sugar. Have you eaten today?" Noah glossed over the obvious cause for the breakdown. He escorted her over to the couch.

"I've eaten," she said, regaining her composure. "I'm so sad and confused lately. I feel like I'm all alone in this." The tears returned to Donna's eyes, but she no longer cared who was watching.

"Donna, have you taken the pills your doctor prescribed?" Noah was speaking in an unfamiliar delicate tone. Donna assumed this is how doctors talk to crazy people. Like he sat through some class in med school just practicing this skill.

"No, I don't want to take a pill to stop feeling this way. I want my daughter back. I want my husband to talk to me again. Some pill is not going to fix my broken life. Don't you understand that?" She looked at Noah as if he were stupid, ignorant for thinking a pill was the solution.

"Do you want to go to the hospital?" Noah asked, and Donna was unsure if it was a question or a threat.

"No," she said, defeated. It was clear Noah wouldn't wrap his arms around her, bury his head in her silvery blonde hair, and join her in sobbing for lost Rayanne. She missed her daughter in a way that maybe no one else on this planet ever could. "I'm fine." She shook off the shroud of sorrow, giving him what he wanted. She stood, cleared her throat, and pushed the conversation forward.

"Why are you here? Did you need something?" She was cold now, tired of being the only one left in this world with chaotic emotions.

"I have a box of Rayanne's things you didn't take when you cleaned the house. I thought you should have them. Some postcards, letters, and books."

"Okay. Just bring it in and put it on the table. I'll go through it later." She wanted to move toward him, stare into his dark eyes, and slap his freshly shaven cheek. She wished she were a stronger woman who could clench a fist and break a nose, but her hand would surely not withstand the blow. Her mind screamed, *I left you that box because you have given me everything else of hers and seem to want nothing to remember her by. Why must I house everything my daughter ever touched, so you can continue on with your life as though none of this happened? You're scrubbing your hands free of Ray's memory, the way you scrub before an operation to rid yourself of germs.*

Staring intensely at him, Donna realized the toll of the accident did show on his face. For a moment she had a hopeful glimmer that his life and heart were shredded to unmanageable pieces, and this cool indifference was all an act. Why she wanted him to hurt so badly she wasn't sure.

She remembered back to her daughter's wedding day. Noah, tall and confident, stood at the end of the aisle, awaiting his bride. She remembered how dark his hair was, slicked back and crisp. She recalled the brightness in his eyes and the glow in his olive skin. Noah was a beautiful man with strong hands, solid legs, and a chiseled jawline.

Now as Donna looked him over, she realized all of those things had faded. He had exercised his mass away. She assumed a combination of not eating and running endlessly on the treadmill were the culprits. His jawline now looked box-like under his thin pale skin, and the lines between his furrowed brows were deep and permanent. His shiny, jet-black hair had turned slowly to a dull charcoal gray with unkempt locks cut too short to be stylish.

She was not looking at a well-rested man. This was not a man who ate, or exercised, in any well-maintained healthy fashion.

"I better get going. Try to make an appointment with the doctor if you're not feeling better by this afternoon." Noah moved toward the door like a rat fleeing a sinking ship.

Donna smiled goodbye. She heard him scurry to the car, drop the box on the table, and move quickly back outside.

She had promised herself she would not run to the box and immerse herself in her daughter's belongings. She had grown very familiar with this process and knew it to be as pleasurable as it was painful. But like a shark drawn to the scent of blood, she was pulled to the kitchen. She lifted the folded edges of the box and let the recognizable smell of her daughter's belongings overtake her.

She moved the books and CDs to the side of the box and instead reached for the more interesting floral patterns toward the bottom. Pulling them out, she realized they were journals. Opening one, she recognized her daughter's handwriting and closed the book tightly. These were her daughter's personal journals, her precious, innermost thoughts and emotions, chronicled in these pages. *I have no right. She's gone. Let it be.* Donna sat for a moment, stunned by the thought of it. She pulled six similar books from the bottom of the box and began to read.

Chapter Seven

Autumn sat in the now familiar living room of Tanya Jones. She was the grief counselor Mike had insisted she see while he was getting treatment in Texas. The room was cramped and the semi-circle of mismatched chairs was filled with solemn faces. A man Autumn knew simply as "Joe" was talking, though his cracking and quivering voice had begun to fail him.

"He was nine," Joe said, wiping his eyes with his hand. "He loved boats and the ocean. My wife and I thought it would be nice to rent a boat and pack a picnic. I only had one job that day, watch the weather. My wife packed the picnic, rented the damn boat, and got us all ready to go. The owner was out of town, but she had arranged everything. She always had everything all planned out. I had the luxury of just showing up most of the time. I mean, I'd carry the heavy stuff, or get things off the top shelf, but she did everything else." Joe paused, letting a hiccup stall his story.

"I'd only really driven boats two or three times, but I'm a damned good mechanic and a man, so I'm just supposed to understand those things. We went out too far, got a little turned around, and by the time the storm rolled in, we were lost. I did what I could, I called the Coast Guard over the radio, but by the time they got to us, it was too late. The boat had capsized; it had pulled my family under and knocked me unconscious. I had a life jacket, just like them, but I hadn't gotten caught up in the debris of the boat." He struck his head with his fist in a guilt-filled rage so suddenly that Autumn rocked backward.

Joe was unable to continue his story, and Tanya came over to him. She waved everyone else out of the room, and most people seemed happy to leave. Joe had been coming to the meetings longer than Autumn. She had been to one a week for the last two months, and she heard Joe say he had been coming for over six months. This was the first time he had told his tragic story. It had taken him six months to even talk in this group. That made Autumn feel slightly better as she had not uttered a single word besides her name to anyone but Tanya. Though the thought of feeling like Joe in four months was not all that appealing.

Autumn had made her way to leave, hoping her cab driver would be early. She had quit driving. Her car hadn't moved since the day of the accident, and while a cab ride was more expensive, she found an immense amount of security in the back seat.

She had not asked the driver to return for another twenty-five minutes. Calling another cab would take at least ten minutes and then the driver she originally asked to return would do so for no reason. She decided to wait it out on the front porch.

People from the group moved past her. There was an old widower named Buck, a young mother named Sue whose son had drowned in a neighbor's pool, and a man named Doug who lost his parents in a plane crash. As Autumn watched the rest of the group file out, she realized she knew all of their stories. They had all shared their pain and their tragedy. All except her, and the last man to exit Tanya's house. She knew his name was Jamie but had heard nothing of his story. She thought he was about twenty and probably in college. He came alone, left alone, and never said a word.

As everyone else left, the cries of Joe the mechanic leaked eerily out the front door. She was glad to see the last of the group trail out, the door finally shutting behind them. She breathed in the night air and watched them all hop in their cars and drive away. All had left except Jamie, who lingered on the porch with no apparent purpose.

"Hey," he coughed out to Autumn, confirming his age by the youthful tone of his voice. He portrayed an aggressive indifference with that one word.

"Hello," she replied, checking her watch and praying, like she always did these days, this did not become some in-depth conversation.

"So we're it now. Joe cracked, and we're the only two left here who haven't given our tragic sob stories." He spoke with no filter. Autumn was stung by his frankness and imagined the words running out of control at full speed from his brain to his mouth.

"Uh-huh," she said, not sure how to respond to his odd statement. She pretended to search through her purse for something, though she had kept nothing of any use in it for months.

"I have to come here. It's court ordered, but I don't have to talk. They can't force me to do that," he groaned back, shaking his head victoriously, as though he had beaten the system. "Why are you here? Court ordered?" He had a note of hopefulness in his voice as though not wanting to be the only one who had been forced to come.

"No," she said, half laughing. "Not court ordered. I was in a car crash, and my husband was killed. I promised his father, who is very ill, that I would come," she said, still digging in her purse.

"So it's not court ordered, but it's not really by choice either. You're here 'cause of guilt," he said smugly, as though he had pegged the situation correctly.

"I guess," she surrendered, admitting to herself that if it weren't for Mike she wouldn't come to these meetings. She wasn't finding any value in attending, and she sure wasn't feeling any better.

"I don't see the point in them. It's depressing. How is hearing everyone else's bullshit supposed to make you feel better? I guess they want you to sit there and say, 'At least I'm not as bad off as that poor slob.' I think it's stupid." Jaime ran his fingers through his blond hair and looked curiously at her. "Did you lose your keys or something?"

She stopped looking through her purse, realizing it had gone on too long and was not preventing the man from wanting to speak to her.

"No, I'm actually just waiting for a cab. We let out early so it'll be a few more minutes before he's back," she explained, finally putting her purse back over her shoulder and sitting down on the steps.

"I'll wait with you," he offered. Autumn was both agitated and intrigued by the idea. She said nothing and allowed him to sit by her.

Jamie smelled like a young man's cologne, sprayed on too thickly, mixing poorly with the smell of his gel or aftershave.

"I'm Jamie, and you're Autumn, right?" he asked, confidently shaking her hand. He seemed to want to drive every conversation, quickly, and to the point.

"Yes," she replied curtly, still feeling so strange about their interaction. She let him continue the conversation, curious to where his young mind might take it.

"So why can't you drive? Did you cause the accident or something? DUI?" he asked, obviously thinking nothing of the festering wound he might be opening.

"No," she answered sharply. "I just prefer a cab." She was now leaning toward the idea that this man had no couth or understanding of how to engage other people, especially grieving people. And every time he spoke he seemed less like a man and more like a child.

"I just thought maybe you had your license taken away, but hey, whatever," he said, shrugging his shoulders at her reaction as though she were being crazy. "You have any kids?" Jamie continued. "Did they die too?"

"Jesus, kid!" Autumn said in a huff. "You don't just go around asking people those kinds of things. What's your damn story? Why are you here?" She stared accusingly, as though he didn't deserve to be a part of the group.

"Sorry, lady. I was just trying to have a conversation," he defended as he stood up. "I guess I'll see you next week." He pulled his keys from his pocket and waved goodbye. His sandy blond hair hung over his blue eyes, and Autumn felt a curious ember of heat begin to build inside her. There was something about this guy she wished to know more about. His questions had agitated her, but his wave goodbye and his small mannerisms intrigued her.

"Wait," she yelled, perhaps too loud and eager. "I'm sorry. I'm just not used to those types of questions. You don't have to go. Please . . . stay." She waved him back and patted the space on the steps beside her.

"That's because everyone around you probably treats you like you are made of glass. They talk all slow and soft, avoiding all the tough subjects. I hate that stuff, so I don't do it. If I'm going to talk to someone it's going to be about exactly what I want; life's too short for all the formalities." He sat back down next to her.

"So why haven't you spoken when you're in the group? Why are you here?" She agreed with the logic of life being too short and decided to take a similar approach with him.

"Well, that's a whole different story. I don't talk in the group because I don't want to. The things I've been through suck, and I'm dead set against dealing with them in a room full of total strangers. However, the court systems seem to feel that my 'inability to coexist and function normally within society' has everything to with the fact that I don't spill my guts before a group of sobbing strangers. You on the other hand must have a ton of family and friends. Why don't you just talk to them instead of coming here?" Autumn noticed he had redirected the conversation back to her. She imagined he had perfected this avoidance technique, and that most people were much happier discussing themselves than listening to others. She allowed him the sanctuary of his diversion.

"I don't have anyone. My parents and I aren't close, and I don't have any siblings. I don't work anymore, so my friends have kind of moved forward without me. My husband was really my best friend, so there aren't a lot of people I can talk to. How about you, why don't you talk to your family or friends?" she asked, taking back control of the conversation.

"I don't have any family, and it's hard to keep friends when you go through stuff because they don't know how to react. They get all weird, and then eventually I think it's easier for them to just stop calling." She heard the sadness in his voice erupt and then quickly subside. She inexplicably yearned to know everything about him. He was deeper than she originally gave him credit for. Knowing he was hurting made the thought of talking to him strangely more appealing.

"I guess that's true. My friends definitely aren't sure how to deal with me. I've been kind of a shut-in," she admitted. "I have a really hard time getting out of bed and doing anything. I used to be so driven, and now I feel like a lump." She put her elbows on her knees and her chin in her hands. "I just wish I could go back to before." Her eyes filled with tears, and soon salty trails were blazing down her face. She felt hot with embarrassment but helpless to stop her emotions.

"You can't," he said quietly with a shrug. "There's no reset button here. You can't rewind and go back, so just get used to it. I don't cry about my stuff. It won't do me any good. But I have something that might." He reached into his shirt pocket and pulled out a flask. As he unscrewed the cover, her eyes stung at the smell of the potent concoction he waved under her nose. "It makes me feel better." He smiled and offered the drink to her.

"No," she said disappointingly. "That's not going to help either. Sitting around and crying won't do it, but drinking definitely isn't going to bring anyone back."

Jamie shrugged his shoulders and took a long swig. He squinted his eyes, and muscled the foul mixture down his throat.

"Are you even old enough to drink?" She felt a maternal responsibility suddenly wash over her.

"Almost, but they drug test me every week, so this is all I have." He let out a quiet breathy laugh that Autumn recognized as defeat.

"Shouldn't your cab be here by now?" Jamie asked, checking his wrist and realizing he hadn't worn a watch.

"Yeah, but I'll just go call another one. I asked the driver to come back, but you know how that goes." Autumn stood and pulled her cell phone from her purse.

"I can give you a lift if you'd like." Jamie pointed to his car. It was red, like Charlie's, except much more expensive looking. It had every bit of chrome Autumn imagined you could buy for a car. She thought of the reckless adolescent, half drunk and driving wildly through the town.

"No," she answered too quickly to be anything less than rude. "I mean, you're drinking. You shouldn't even be driving. Why don't we share a cab, and you come back for your car tomorrow?" She tried to make her case with a note of concern evident in her voice.

"Nah." He waved his hand at her. "I can handle myself." He dug in his pocket again for his car keys, and Autumn's eyes watered—partly from the thought of her husband and partly from the potency of Jamie's breath. She wasn't sure what was coming over her. She pictured the red car split in half, Jamie ejected through the windshield.

"No, you can't go." She was certain Jamie would react poorly to her seizing control. After all, he was being forbidden to do something. It was clear he was one of those people who rebelled against commands. She took a different approach. "It's been good talking with you. Maybe we could get some coffee or something." The reaction on Jamie's face made it clear to Autumn she had not thought this plan through enough.

"Listen, Autumn, you're a nice lady and all, but you're old enough to be my mother. I don't think it would work out between us. You're kind of hot for your age and all, but—"

Autumn cut across his word incredulously.

"No! I don't mean like that. I just thought we could both use a break or whatever. Don't flatter yourself, kid." She felt like a child, mortified and slashing back at an attack. She wanted to reveal her real intention. She wanted to tell the cocky young brat who just called her old and desperate that her real objective was to give him time to sober up before driving.

"Oh, well okay, I guess." He still looked skeptical, but his face revealed slight embarrassment. He shrugged again, and Autumn imagined that was his most common form of communication.

When the cab arrived Autumn felt her stomach fill with regret. What had she thought, asking this man-child for coffee? Even if her intention were merely to help, what would people think? What would they talk about? Would she be able to stomach his crude frankness and socially inept behavior for the duration of a cup of coffee? It was too late to back out, and as she flopped into the cab, she decided to let herself fall into the moment and be swept her away.

Just this once.

* * * *

"I'll have a caramel mocha latte, heavy on the cream and sugar," Jamie said, not offering to let Autumn order first. His lack of manners was trumped only by his choice of drink, which Autumn realized was for someone who enjoyed saying they loved coffee, but truly hated the taste. He was merely showing off.

"I'll just have a medium regular," Autumn said, smiling blankly at the bored waitress, who snapped her gum and walked away without so much as an acknowledgement of their presence.

"So, your husband, was he a good guy? I mean everyone who dies becomes some kind of martyr saint thing, but was he really a good guy?" Jamie hadn't looked up at her as he asked the question. It wasn't because he was uncomfortable with the callousness, but because he was intently stacking sugar packets like a house of cards.

"Well, he was kind and smart. He had a way of saying the right thing at just the right moment, and no matter what I was feeling he would bend and shape to whatever I needed. He could anticipate my emotions and worked hard to makes sure I had everything." She smiled at the bland face of the waitress who had returned and dropped two cups of coffee in front of them.

"That's cool. I think I'm a lot like that too. I mean I drink and smoke, and I guess I don't always make the right choices, but I'm a good person." He pulled a pack of cigarettes from his pocket and shook one out into his hand.

"And you're modest too," she said, becoming less sure of why she was here. This half boy/half man had some serious problems and while she enjoyed the distraction, she questioned her reasons.

"Yeah, I'm that too," he said, clearly not listening. "I try to do the right thing, but it's hard. People just seem to expect me to screw up, and I keep proving them right." He sipped his coffee, and for brief a moment, Autumn saw a flash of vulnerability that vanished as quickly as it had come.

"What do you mean?" she probed, trying to look uninterested, though she was actually quite curious. Jamie was clearly filled with inner turmoil. He had all the signs and symptoms of someone who had been tossed aside like yesterday's trash.

He sighed and abruptly put his coffee cup on the table. "You know, people just look at me and see a worthless punk, so it's easier to just be a punk. They see a screw-up, so here I am screwing up. No one cares what happens to me; they just want something to talk about. They want someone who is worse off than them, so when they lay down at night they can sleep well. Every doctor, every grief counselor, every foster parent," he counted them out on his fingers. "They just want to know there is someone out there more fucked up than they are." He sat back in the booth of the old coffee shop and crossed his arms, slumping in rejected defeat.

"It's pretty sad how bitter you are. You're far too young to be so pissed at the world, so jaded. I hope that changes for you someday soon, Jamie. I hope you don't feel like this forever." Autumn was speaking straight from her heart. She didn't dress it up. She didn't try to fix it or persuade Jamie otherwise. A small gratitude smile was a surprise to see.

"Thanks. I don't want to feel like this forever either. It's just all I've got right now." He sniffed, and Autumn reached across the table for his hand, covering it with hers.

"Thanks for coming here with me. I literally haven't been anywhere voluntarily since the accident. I've been to appointments and grocery shopping, but I haven't been anywhere without being forced to go. Today was," she hesitated, realizing he might not be the right audience for her pain, "it just wasn't a good day, you know?" She released his hand, feeling silly, slapping on a fake smile as she waved away his look of pity.

"Yeah, I know what you mean. Hey, this kept me from drinking and driving, for tonight anyway, so it worked out for both of us." He chuckled uncomfortably.

They'd sat in the booth for over an hour, ordering a refill now and then. The waitress was clearly annoyed they wouldn't be ordering any food and had disappeared.

They didn't really talk about anything. They discussed small things, like TV shows they both used to like and Las Vegas. Autumn had been with Charlie years ago, and Jamie lit up, swearing he would live there one day.

"Let's get a cab back to your car and call it a night," Autumn suggested, reaching for her purse.

"Why don't we drop you off first, it's pretty late to be taking a cab alone," Jamie suggested. Autumn was shocked at his thoughtfulness.

"Thanks, I might take you up on that. It is pretty late, and I haven't had the most upstanding cab drivers lately."

Chapter Eight

It was six days before Autumn realized the mistake she had made. At the time she thought nothing would come from Jamie knowing where she lived. Her mind couldn't sink low enough to imagine any darkness coming from this sad misguided guy, but her gut was wrong.

She awoke from her familiar car accident dream to hear a loud pounding at her door. When she finally composed herself the banging had stopped, and for a moment she thought perhaps she had dreamed it. Then a tap on her window grew to a pounding that rattled the wall. It was accompanied by the deep whisper of a strange voice.

"Autumn, are you there?" the voice slurred. "Autumn, you gotta let me in," he called again between the relentless banging.

Autumn slipped on her husband's robe, which she had recently begun placing under the covers beside her. She pulled back the curtain, slipped her fingers between the blinds, and peered out into the darkness. "Jamie?" she asked with disbelief. "Go to the door and for the love of God, stop banging."

As Autumn moved down the stairs toward the front door she thought for a brief second of her safety. Did she really even know Jamie? Should she call the police? What would Charlie have her do? All valid questions, but there was no time to answer them. She couldn't very well have Jamie start banging on the door again, waking the neighbors, who already thought she'd gone insane.

She unlocked the door, pulled it open, and stood rigidly in her doorway. She looked Jamie over and saw he was not bleeding or injured. What he did have was deep hurt in his eyes.

"What is it, Jamie? What are you doing here? It's the middle of the night." She hadn't welcomed him in, but before she had finished her last syllable he was moving past her, looking paranoid and lost. He pulled Autumn in, and she stiffened further at his rough warm hand on hers. He quickly shut the door and put his finger to his lips, telling her to be quiet. Flipping off the light she had turned on, he crept on his muddy shoes into her kitchen.

"Jamie, what's wrong? Is someone following you? Are you in trouble?" Autumn flipped the light on, and Jamie threw his hands up as if to say, "Come on, you're ruining everything." He sighed and finally spoke.

"Fine, turn the lights on, but he's gonna find me. I don't know how, but he always tracks me down. And then it's all over." Jamie exaggerated his words, and even without the pungent stink of bourbon, it would have been easy to tell he was drunk. Autumn shook her head and peered out her kitchen window. She was curious about who was following Jamie and if they were both in any danger. Examining her front lawn, all she saw was Jamie's flashy car skewed across the grass. Luckily the lawn was dead; it had gone unkempt for so long the ostentatious vehicle parked across it actually made it look better.

Autumn turned backed to Jamie. He was sitting awkwardly on a bar stool in her kitchen. She crossed her arms, raised an eyebrow, and said in a stern tone, "You have thirty seconds to tell me what's going on, or I'm throwing you out." She looked at the clock over her fridge and intended to give him exactly thirty seconds. To her surprise he didn't speak. He slumped forward onto her counter and his head began swaying heavily. As the end of his thirty seconds ticked away, there was a quiet knock at her door.

Autumn's lungs flooded with gravel as her throat seized up. Perhaps there was someone after Jamie, and now they were both in trouble. Her mind racing, she wondered: Did I lock the door? Is it too late?

"There he is." Jamie's words garbled together. "Now we're both screwed." He raised his head for a moment and then plopped it back onto the cool granite of Autumn's countertop. Jamie was out cold.

Autumn moved to the door, grabbed the fireplace poker, and slung it up on her shoulder like a soldier's sword. She peered through the door's peephole, holding her breath. For a moment, she imagined an angry mob of villagers on the other side with pitchforks and torches. Instead there was just one man fidgeting nervously. He looked as though, at any moment, he might bolt. Oddly, something inside Autumn didn't want him to. He had a look on his face that made a hundred questions swirl in her mind.

She watched him through the door for a long moment. He looked from side to side nervously. He was clearly contemplating if he should knock again or just leave. She saw him move backward down the top step.

Autumn heard herself whisper, "Wait." She placed her hand on the coolness of her front door. The metal of the fire poker slipped and clanked clumsily against it.

"Hello?" the man asked, springing back to the top step. "Jamie, is that you?" He pressed himself close against the door.

"Who are you?" Autumn snapped in a deeper voice than she meant to. "What do you want?" She clenched the makeshift weapon tighter in her hand and straightened her back. She thought back to the two self-defense classes she had taken and tried to remember her eye jabs and foot stomps.

She watched the man cover his mouth and raise his shoulders in embarrassment. He again stepped down one step and then another.

She swung the door open and pointed the fire poker in the stranger's direction. "Hey," she called to him, "who are you?" She hardly recognized her own voice. It was demanding and formidable. She liked the way this power tasted on her tongue. For the second time in one night, she began a countdown.

"You've got ten seconds to tell me what the hell you are doing on my front steps in the middle of the night." She didn't have an "or else" statement lined up, but she felt it was obvious by the tone of her voice.

The man eyed the fire poker and the blaze roaring in her eyes. He was clearly searching for words that wouldn't seem to come, and Autumn began to feel sorry for him as if he was lost somehow, if not physically, then mentally.

Finally he spoke. "My name is Travis. I was looking for . . ." he trailed off and pointed to the car that sat abandoned on Autumn's lawn.

"Why, what do you want with him?"

"I'm his AA sponsor among other things," Travis explained, still trying to maintain a discrete whisper.

"Well you're doing a pretty shitty job. He's inside, drunk off his ass, passed out at my counter." She moved aside and waved Travis in, hoping he could relieve her of the drooling heap in her kitchen.

Travis rolled his neck as though his head was screwed on too tight and the pressure was unbearable.

"Oh, Jamie." Travis sighed and entered the house as if this kind of scene had worn permanent ruts in his brain but still had a disappointing sting.

Travis turned back to Autumn, checking to see if she had put down her weapon. "Ma'am, I'm very sorry for the intrusion."

"Wait," Autumn said incredulously. "So let me get this straight, I've got a car ruining my lawn, a drunk kid drooling on my counter, a stranger banging on my door in the middle of the night, and now you're going to call me ma'am? What a night." She tossed the fire poker back in its metal holster, jumping slightly at the loud noise the impact made.

"Sorry," Travis apologized, biting his lip. "I'll get him up, and we'll be out of your hair in no time." Travis moved toward Jamie and pulled him to a sitting position. Jamie's head rolled backward. He was clearly not going to be leaving by his own volition.

"He's out cold. You're not going to wake him." She sighed, feigning frustration. If she were being honest with herself she was thrilled to have commotion in her quiet house once again. Loneliness had become a bubble she'd slipped inside, and every now and then she wanted to break free.

"I can carry him out and drive him home. It won't be the first time. I don't want to keep you up any longer." He attempted to pull the stool away from counter in order to get a better angle to lift Jamie.

She watched his bicep flex and caught herself staring. Autumn realized suddenly she was in a dirty robe with a messy knot of hair at the top of her head. It had been months since she had cared about her appearance, and now it hit her like a bolt of lightning how terrible she must look. While Travis had his back to her, she tried to smooth her hair to some semblance of style.

"Just leave him," she insisted as she watched Travis struggle to rein in the drunken mess. "Let's give him time to sober up. Would you like some coffee?" she asked, already filling the pot with water.

"I don't want to put you out, but if you're making a pot, that would be great." He wiped his forehead and rubbed his eyes in what looked to Autumn like pure exhaustion.

"It's no problem. It looks like Jamie can be a handful. I don't envy you." She pulled two mugs from the cabinet, something she hadn't done since her husband had died.

This man in her kitchen didn't look a thing like Charlie. Travis was a bit shorter, his nose was crooked, but it only made his face more interesting. He had just the right amount of hair on his chin, walking that fine line between attractive and homeless. His hair was thick and dark. It fell to the left and right without any rhyme or reason, yet looked very trendy. His eyes were green, not emerald or ivy, but the green of weathered sea glass. Autumn wondered how old he was; she guessed somewhere between thirty and thirty-five.

"How do you know Jamie? He hasn't mentioned you." Travis was peeking over at Jamie to make sure he wasn't about to fall off the stool.

"We're in the same grief group. Last week he had been drinking, so I took him out for a cup of coffee. We took a cab, and I was dropped off first. I guess he remembered where I lived and came back. He's a pretty troubled kid, huh?" Autumn pulled the cream from the fridge, the sugar from the counter, and placed them in front of Travis, who was now sitting on the stool next to Jamie.

"Yeah. He's been through a lot. I just wish I knew how to help him. I met him in the court system five years ago. He had been through three foster homes and was on the verge of being placed in a halfway house until he was eighteen. He's the poster child for an unwanted kid. It broke my heart. My wife and I had been foster parents years before, and I thought I could make a difference in his life." Travis fiddled with the button at the top of his shirt as though it were choking him.

As the word "wife" passed over his lips it sprung across the kitchen and slapped Autumn in the face. She felt an unmistakable, unwarranted pang of jealousy and disappointment. This man had burst into her life ten minutes ago, who was she to be jealous?

"I moved him in, signed him up for grief groups, got him back in school, and tried to be there for him." Travis looked over at Jamie and sighed. Disenchantment danced at the corner of his eyes, and for a moment the glimmer of a tear seemed to form but rapidly disappeared.

"He hasn't told me what happened, so I'm not really sure how he ended up in foster care to begin with." Autumn turned her gaze to Jamie as if trying to stare into him and read his mind.

"Well, I'm not one to tell anyone else's story. I know he's tried to put it behind him, but I will say it's one of the worst stories I've ever heard. Before my wife died, we had plenty of foster children with some pretty tough histories, but Jamie has the bad luck market cornered." Travis rubbed the corner of his almond shaped eyes and yawned.

"What happened to your wife? I only ask because I recently lost my husband in a car accident." Autumn ran her finger around the rim of her coffee mug and avoided Travis's eyes as if he were Medusa, threatening to turn her to stone.

"Cancer," he said as he poured some cream into his coffee and took a long swig. "I guess that's really what drove me to take Jamie in. I was hurting and lonely, and so was he. If life were a TV movie, this would have all worked out perfectly by now. Unfortunately, I stayed sad, he started drinking, and I'm not sure either one of us is any better off."

"I'm sorry to hear about your wife, and I'm even sorrier to hear that the sadness hasn't subsided. I'm not sure I can be in this state too much longer. I thought it would get better with time, like everyone kept insisting it would, but at least you're being honest with me." Autumn nibbled at the inside of her cheek as she thought about the many years ahead of her where this sadness would envelope her very being.

"I'm sorry to be the bearer of bad news," Travis apologized. "I guess it's different for everyone though. I manage to get through the day, and there are moments I don't feel so . . ." He shrugged away the thought.

Autumn tried to fill in the blank. "It feels like I'm seven years old again, and I've just been bundled into my snowsuit, boots, hat, and gloves, but instead of heading outside to play in the snow, I'm just walking through life bound up in these suffocating clothes, waiting for something to happen." She saw Travis's mouth open to respond, but she cut in, not done with her thoughts. "Grief is like a paper cut or a toothache of emotion. It's dull but constant. It's relentless. Maybe you can take something to help the ache, but you know it's there waiting for you when all the medication and distractions have disappeared. When the room is quiet and the lights are off, it's just you and your grief." She didn't mean to say all that. Surely Travis didn't come here to listen to a stranger ramble on about her idea of pain. But she decided to keep going until he stopped her or she ran out of things to say.

"What I hate is that people don't get it. If someone thinks there should be a time limit to feeling like this, all that tells me is they've never had to struggle with it themselves. It's not just some intangible state of being. I can taste it; it tastes metallic and sour, and it makes everything I used to eat feel like sand in my mouth. I can see it too. It's murky water and windless hot days. Everything I had, knew, or believed died in that car, and I'm just some half-human, half-zombie, waiting for something to change." She closed her eyes somewhere in the middle of her statement and was now sitting silently with cool tears rolling down her cheeks.

Travis grunted and nodded his head in agreement. "I've spent five years trying to say those words. Maybe not those exact words," he chuckled as he covered her hand with his for a brief heart-stopping moment, "but I have felt every piece of what you just said. I have tasted it, woken up next to it, and run from it. I've been right where you are; maybe I'm still there." He breathed in, closed his eyes, and dropped his head down in defeat.

"I will never stop loving my wife and wishing every day she were back. But it's exhausting to love someone who can't hear about my day or make fun of my terrible taste in movies." He propped his elbows on the granite and rested his head in his hands. "I would love to tell you that someday you'll stop closing your eyes and begging and bargaining with God to bring him back, but I haven't come to that day yet, and it's been years. I still sit quietly at times and tell God if he brings her back, I won't make a fuss or ask any questions. I'll pretend nothing happened and just go back to my life the way it was. I'm not sure I'll ever stop hoping for that."

"What the hell is this?" Autumn started laughing in a silly and fanatical tone. "We met half an hour ago and here we are, bleeding hearts with tears in our eyes. This is my life now. I have these grief groups where the whole point is for me to go

53

there and just listen to people who are hurting so badly. I swear sometimes I'm sitting there listening and wondering how is this sadness therapy? It just makes me want to . . ." Autumn's sentence went unfinished as an unsettling gurgle bubbled out of Jamie's drooling mouth. A stream of rainbow-colored vomit splattered to the kitchen tile.

"Exactly!" Autumn said, beginning to cackle again at the random events and bizarre conversations this night and these strangers had brought. It was marginally better than being alone.

Chapter Nine

"Dr. Key," a nurse whispered as the door to the small on-call room opened and the noises of the emergency room spilled in, "I'm sorry to wake you but—"

Noah cut into her words, "It's fine." He hadn't been asleep anyway. Going in the on-call room and shutting off the light was all for show. He'd been told by a colleague to leave the emergency room to get some rest; he'd been on a shift for the last twenty hours. That was the problem working with doctors. They understood the impact of sleep deprivation, and all eyes were on him lately. It was easier to do as he was told before someone caught on to what was really going on with him.

It had become an art over the last few months. He'd managed to pick up so many shifts he almost never had to leave the hospital. The other perk: he got all the best cases. All while avoiding the suffocating reality that waited on the other side of the emergency room doors. Only eating to survive and sleeping just before his body gave out was a delicate balance but it worked. People had begun to take notice of his weight loss and black-rimmed exhausted eyes but his gruff demeanor lately had kept them at bay. It was amazing what becoming a widower could buy in the way of forgiveness for being a complete asshole to people. They'd judge him, but when they remembered his loss, pity would roll in.

She spoke again, this time slightly louder. "Dr. Munro said to wake you. There was a train derailment, and they're expecting multiple traumas rolling in any minute. It's all hands on deck." The nurse had a mousy nervousness as though she'd drawn the short straw to be sent into the lion's den.

"Got it," Noah answered with a grunt. He sprang to a sitting position and slipped his feet back into his shoes. Flipping on the light, he pulled on his white doctor's coat and draped his stethoscope around his neck. A train accident would keep him busy for the rest of the night. No one would give him a hard time about how tired he looked, because by the end of this everyone working would be exhausted. He'd be able to coast right through Tuesday. Or was it Wednesday? As much as he didn't want to admit it, his memory was beginning to be affected by the lack of sleep. Paired with a limited amount of food and excessive exercising, he knew he was punishing his body. But there was something fitting about that. He deserved to pay for what he'd done.

When he pulled open the door to the on-call room and stepped out into the hallway his adrenaline took over. He was running on fumes, but the energy that soared through the emergency room during a trauma situation was enough to keep him going. The first stretcher rolled by with a patient suffering a serious head wound, and he had to fight off a smile. None of his demons would have a chance to whisper in his ear tonight, he'd be far too busy for that.

Chapter Ten

Autumn passed the money through the small window to the cab driver and stared at the house where the grief group had gathered. Stepping out, she craned her neck to evaluate each car lined up in front. Mostly the regulars who never missed a week of counseling, but she took note of a few new cars. Jamie's flashy red car was nowhere to be seen. Travis had pulled Jamie out of her kitchen, wedged him in the backseat of his car, and drove off; she wasn't sure she'd see either of them again. And she didn't know why she cared.

Jamie had been smug and reckless with his words, but there was something about him that cut through his brash exterior. Travis had been kind and apologetic, and she found some kindred feelings in how he'd been beat up by life. These were the first two people since Charlie's death she felt might actually understand how she felt. It was like they'd all been knocked off their axis and, while the rest of the world couldn't really see the subtle way they leaned to one side, they could recognize it in each other.

She climbed the front steps and let herself in the way she always did. The group was already chatting and filling their coffee cups; she passed into the living room and took a seat. A familiar arrogant voice rose up from behind her. "I puked on your kitchen floor didn't I?" Jamie asked, leaning in over her shoulder.

She nodded, offered a tiny smile, and turned in her chair to face him. A rush of relief passed over her, knowing she wasn't alone in this sea of people. "I didn't think you were coming. Your car wasn't out front."

"Travis stole my keys like he's my dad or something and I missed curfew. I've done some pretty screwed up stuff but this, going to your house and being that drunk, sent him over the edge. He dropped me off today, and he's picking me up later. I happen to think it's just because he wants to see you again." Jamie's lips curled up devilishly, and he winked.

"What?" she asked with a huff. "What is that supposed to mean?"

"I think he likes you." Jamie shrugged. "He was pissed I'd barged in your house and was all worried about you. I've known him a while, and I've never seen him like that before."

"Maybe he's just tired of you being an idiot," she countered with a hiss. Jamie hadn't said anything overtly insulting, but he clearly wasn't getting the seriousness of his stupid suggestion.

"I've always been an idiot, but the way he says your name, I think there is really something there. He's a great guy, like a saint; trust me. I think if you gave him a chance you'd be good together."

Any ounce of warmth or kindred spirit she felt toward Jamie evaporated like a drop of dew on a hot summer morning. She had to use all her strength not to strike him across his insensitive face. "I just lost my husband," she chirped out. "I don't want to *like* another man. I want my husband back. If Travis thinks now is a good time to start a relationship, then he's the idiot; if he sent you in here to talk to me about it, then you're both cruel. You can tell Travis I'm not interested, and I'll find a new grief group next week."

"Autumn," Jamie stammered, clearly not expecting this reaction. "Travis didn't send me in here, and he's not that kind of guy or anything."

Autumn stood and crossed the room to a new chair where she was sandwiched between two brand new faces. An older woman was clutching rosary beads on her left, and a man with short blond hair who looked about her age was on her right. She averted her eyes away from Jamie and took the hot cup of coffee the man next to her offered even though she didn't want it. She turned toward him in order to turn away from Jamie and began chatting cordially with him until the meeting formally began.

She already knew she wouldn't speak this week. Over the last few weeks, and even at today's meeting, she'd casually mentioned her husband had died months earlier in a car accident, but it was all she was willing to share. Her emotions were raked over hot coals as she thought of Jamie's complete lack of sensitivity. All she wanted to do was go home, crawl in bed, and stare at her ceiling.

When the meeting wrapped up, she lingered in the living room waiting for Jamie to leave. In order to appear completely unavailable for a counter argument, she continued to engage Paul, the sandy haired man she had sat next to in order to escape Jamie's idiocy.

"This seems like a good group," Paul said as everyone else began to disperse. "I've been to some that are just too much, you know?"

She nodded her head and peeked at her watch to see how much longer until her cab would arrive. With any luck Travis would have picked up Jamie by now, and she could put that whole awkward scenario behind her.

"You seem distracted," Paul said, crouching down slightly to grab her gaze. He flashed his too bright white smile at her and tipped his head sideways. "I'm not keeping you am I?"

"No, I'm sorry," Autumn apologized. "I'm actually just waiting for a cab. I think I might head out the back door though. I don't like to chat much with everyone after a meeting."

"I totally understand. I am the exact same way. Do you mind if I come with you? I didn't offer much during this meeting, and being the new guy I know they'll pounce on me if I hang out on the porch."

She was peering toward the front door as he spoke and barely took in what Paul was saying. "Sure," she shrugged and grabbed her purse and headed out back. She'd linger on the side of the house, one eye watching for Travis and Jamie to leave and the other watching for her cab to show up.

"So," Paul said, drawing the words out.

Autumn planted her feet in what seemed like a good spot by some bushes at the corner of the house. Craning her neck, she tried to keep an eye on the road.

"You lost your husband right? That must be tough. Lonely right?" Paul was working hard to get her attention, but she was hardly giving him any until his words started to sink in.

She looked at him curiously, his expression not matching his words. There was no empathy in his eyes, only an unidentifiable glint.

"You just need to feel good, right?" he asked, leaning in close to her ear and whispering through her hair. "I can help you with that."

"I-I, what?" Autumn asked, the cylinders in her brain grinding to a halt, unable to process the situation.

"I know you feel guilty, but your husband isn't here anymore, and you deserve to feel good. I can make you feel good." He reached up and hooked her brown hair in his fingers and tucked it behind her ear. She had the urge to slap his hand away but stopped herself. Surely she was confused, and she'd be mortified if she hit him and then found out this was completely innocent.

"I'm sorry," she said leaning away from him. It was hard to know what the apology was even for. She was sorry if she led him to believe she was looking for something to happen between them. She was sorry for existing as a woman and then turning down his advances.

"No, shh," he said, raising a finger to her lips. She could smell the burnt scent of old cigarette smoke, and suddenly her confusion turned to repulsion with a flicker of fear. "These meetings don't help, do they?" he asked, but didn't wait for her answer. "You're alone every night, just sad and not sure what to do. But we can go back to my place and have some wine. I'm a great listener. Then, just for a little while, I can make you forget everything that's hurting you. Doesn't that sound good?"

His face was inches from hers, and she was furious with herself for not being assertive. There had to be a perfect comeback that would send this guy scurrying away with his tail between his legs. But she couldn't form the words. "I'm going to go," she stuttered out, taking a step back. But like a perverted waltz, he moved in time with her, his body against hers, pressing her to the wall of the house.

"A woman your age isn't going to get many of these offers," he explained, his eyes hardening now as he stared down at her. She didn't stand a chance; if Paul really wanted to hurt her, he could.

Her mind instantly flashed to Charlie. Her husband would never allow something like this to happen. He'd have spotted Paul the moment he entered the room and paid close attention to him. When Paul didn't speak up in the grief meeting, didn't show a single sign of grief at all, Charlie would have noticed. As she stood pinned against the wall, wondering what kind of evil Paul might be, Charlie would have flipped his lid.

It was one of the saddest parts of losing her husband, and it turned from something she couldn't really articulate into something very concise. Charlie would die to protect her. When he was alive there was a person on this earth who would willingly give his life to keep her from harm. Of course the odds it would ever come to that were slim, but there was something wholly comforting about that truth. Now with it gone, she was left vulnerable in so many ways.

"Get off me, please. I'm sorry," she apologized again. "I just want to go. My cab is probably here."

"My place is within walking distance. We can just see where things go," he said softly, bringing his lips to her neck. That had been the breaking point. Her body was a hollow husk. It was a barren wasteland of sorrow—but it was her wasteland.

"Get off me," she shouted, trying to shove him back, but he only drove harder against her. "I'll scream."

"You can scream for me later," he laughed and tried to move her long hair off her neck to gain more access to her skin.

"Autumn," Jamie barked, and Paul spun his head to see who was causing the intrusion. "Are you all right?"

"No," she said, hot tears rolling down her cheeks as she fought to push Paul away again. "No," she repeated, answering Jamie's question but also protesting Paul's touch.

"Get the fuck off her," Jamie shouted as he closed the distance between them. Throwing his shoulder into Paul, he knocked him back.

"What the hell kid, get out of here. This is none of your business." Paul puffed up his chest and made a move toward Autumn. If there was any question in Jamie's mind about whether or not Autumn was afraid, her desperate lunge to get away from Paul told him everything he needed to know.

"I just want to go, Jamie. I just want to leave," she begged, grabbing Jamie's sweatshirt and trying to yank him backward. But, just like Paul, her small frame could not move him.

"What the hell were you doing to her?" Jamie asked, balling his hands into fists and gritting his teeth.

"Don't Jamie," Autumn begged, knowing Paul's odds of winning this fight were great, and Jamie couldn't afford any more trouble.

"Listen kid, there's plenty of other chicks in there you could bag. What about that blonde with the dead sister? She's more your age. I already worked this one up." Paul gestured toward Autumn, and her urge to vomit grew.

Jamie rushed forward and, with a low tackle, brought Paul to the ground. It had been sheer physics that worked in Jamie's favor. He'd gotten under Paul's center of gravity and knocked him down. Surely he'd lose the upper hand. But there was no time to find that out. With a burst of energy from behind her,

Travis came charging past. He grabbed Jamie by the collar and caught his fist before it could plow into Paul's boxy face.

"Jamie, stop," Travis demanded as he wrangled him off Paul. They both stumbled back, gaining their footing. "What the hell are you doing? You are on probation. This is it Jamie, I swear. I can't help you anymore." He turned toward Autumn and shook his head. "Autumn are you all right?"

Paul brushed the dirt off his sweater and got to his feet. Pushing his hair off his forehead and back into place, he grunted out a laugh.

Autumn saw Jamie's anger turn to frustration. It was easy to peg him as the instigator and a screw up, but Autumn wouldn't let that happen.

"Jamie was helping me," Autumn explained as she wiped the remnants of tears away. "Paul, he's, he was trying to . . ." She trailed off and looked at the jerk who couldn't stop smiling.

Paul glared at Autumn arrogantly. "I misjudged you for sure. I had you pegged as a horny depressed lady, but apparently you've got plenty of guys already getting a piece of you. Guess I was just late to the party."

"What?" Travis asked, clearly not piecing all this together yet.

"Don't worry dude," Paul said shooting his arms up in defeat. "I was gonna hit that, but if you've already got claim on it I'll just find some other hot mess to get with. These grief groups are great, and these sad chicks are a dime a dozen. I'll take one with less drama." Paul began to walk away, smart enough not to turn his back on them as he did.

"Wait," Travis called out, putting a hand up to his forehead like he was trying to force the information to his brain. "What's happening here?"

Travis looked from Paul to Jamie but then let his gaze rest on Autumn. Maybe it was the way she was holding her sweater closed so defensively, or the tussled mess that her hair had become, but it took very few words to explain what happened.

"He wouldn't get off me," she croaked out, rolling her eyes back so tears wouldn't start again. That was all it took for all the confusion to be blown away.

Travis's gaze turned from empathy to fury as he charged toward Paul. Unlike Jamie, Travis stood a couple inches taller than Paul, and his shoulders were every bit as wide.

"Whoa buddy, I already said you could have her," Paul explained, putting his hands up to try to keep Travis from making contact with him but to no avail. Travis's right hook made direct contact with Paul's jaw and sent him back to the dirt. As Travis drew his leg back, ready to kick, it was Jamie who was now doing the intervening.

"Travis," Jamie shouted and tried to yank him backward. It wasn't fast enough to keep the kick from connecting, but his interference was enough to at least stop the next blow.

If Travis had the intention of going back for more it was the look on Autumn's face that stopped him. She'd brought her hands up to her mouth and closed her eyes tightly as though she were willing her body to teleport somewhere else. When the commotion stopped, she opened her eyes and saw Travis stepping back, shaking the ache out of his hand. Paul rolled a few feet away from him before standing and wiping the blood from the small cut on his cheek.

"I'm gonna call the cops," Paul barked. He fished his phone out of his pocket with one hand and pointed accusingly at Travis with his other.

"If you don't, I will," Travis countered. "I'm guessing today wasn't the first time you acted like a dickhead, and Autumn isn't the first woman to turn you down. Let's see what kind of record you have and how quickly we can add sexual assault to that."

"Go to hell," Paul shouted, flashing his middle finger at them as he stumbled toward the neighborhood behind the house.

"Should we grab him?" Jamie asked, looking ready to run him down.

"No," Autumn answered first. "I want to go. My cab is probably here. I need to get out of here, and I don't want to deal with what comes when you call the cops. Let's just let it go."

"Your cab left," Jamie said matter-of-factly. "It was sitting there for a few minutes, which is why I came looking for you. When I saw that guy on you I—" Jamie's nose twitched with anger and Travis seemed to know just what to do. With a firm grip on Jamie's shoulder, he brought him back to the moment.

"I'm sorry I assumed you started the fight," Travis apologized sincerely. "I'm glad you were here. Autumn, are you sure you aren't hurt?"

"No," she said quietly, not sure if she was answering that she wasn't hurt, or that she wasn't sure. Before she could clarify, she spun around to the bush at her side and vomited. Shaking with emotion, she braced herself with one hand against the siding of the house and backed her shoes far enough not to get splashed.

She felt a hand on her back and instantly recoiled. Maybe it was the thought of Paul again that made her move away from the touch. Or it was Jamie's earlier words. Travis was a kind man. His large warm hand on her back was comforting, but that was not what Autumn wanted in her life right now. If he liked her, if he wanted more, then he was misguided.

"I'm going to call another cab," she announced and used her sleeve to wipe at the bitter taste in her mouth.

"I'll give you a ride home," Travis insisted as he grabbed his keys and gestured for Jamie to come.

"No," Autumn announced assertively. "You might be the second guy tonight to tell me what I'm going to do, but you'll also be the second guy I answer no to. I hope you're better at listening than Paul."

"Autumn," Travis said, his mouth agape as he searched for the words. "I'm not trying to tell you what to do. I'm so sorry that happened to you tonight; I'm just trying to help."

"I'm not interested in a relationship with you," she spat out as she folded her arms across her chest. "For heaven's sake my husband just died."

"I know," Travis countered. "I'm not offering you an engagement ring; I just thought since you're shaking and puking and scared I might give you a ride home. I hope I didn't imply that I was looking for more."

"You didn't, but . . ." She looked over at Jamie, who was uncharacteristically nervous as he bit at his thumbnail.

"What did you say to her?" Travis asked, looking like he might pummel Jamie. "You didn't seriously stick your nose in my business, did you?"

"She's nice," Jamie defended. "You're nice. You're like the same age, and you both had your spouse die. I just thought if you got together it would be good for you. Both of you."

"You've got to be kidding me, Jamie," Travis said, slapping a hand to his own forehead. "You've got to stop this. Stop acting like a selfish, pigheaded jackass. God, you're no better than—"

"Paul?" Jamie asked, his eyes going wide as he bit down on his lip indignantly. "I'm just some piece of shit guy like him." He made a move to head for the street, blowing by Travis but stopping when Autumn got in his path. He was unable to just dismiss the gentle hand that reached out and touched his chest, his heart, to keep him from passing.

"Jamie," she whispered so only he could hear her, "you are nothing like Paul. Thank you for coming to look for me. Thank you for helping me. We all have our problems. God knows I have plenty right now, but you are nothing like him." She reached up, brought his head down to her shoulder, and pulled him in for a hug. Kissing his cheek before letting him go, she felt him flinch at the unfamiliar gesture.

"I didn't know what I said was going to piss you off," he grunted as he pulled away.

She was tempted to inform him that his words were not a proper apology, but from the look in his eyes she figured what he was offering was the best he could do. There was a time in her life she'd have believed *doing the best you could* was a cop-out. But as her life had spiraled and something as simple as driving her own car became impossible, she was far more willing to accept people's limitations.

"It's okay." She sighed and looked over at the street where her cab was no longer parked. It would take a while for the cab company to send another driver out to her.

"Come get a bite to eat," Jamie suggested. He kicked at some loose dirt and averted his eyes from her.

She felt a protest rise up but held it back, thinking of what Jamie had done for her. He didn't have to come looking for her. He easily could have seen the cab and ignored that she wasn't there. He could have seen Paul, misread the situation, and turned away. He just tackled a man for her. Travis had slugged him, for heaven's sake. Was she really in a position to push any other people away? Lonely felt good most of the time when it was a choice, but at what point would she regret creating complete solitude?

"I'm hungry." She breathed out heavily. "I left my last meal in the bushes."

It had felt like such a very long time since something she said had elicited the response those two little words just had. She'd seen Jamie smirk before. She'd seen him sarcastically grin. But her announcement of hunger had brought on a teeth-showing, eyes-lit-up smile that he flashed seemingly before he remembered not to. It was fleeting and punctuated by hunching his shoulders and stuffing his hands in his pocket as he headed toward the car.

"Let's eat then or whatever," he said, not looking back at them as he walked.

Autumn glanced toward Travis, who looked unsure which emotion to display. He looked relieved, stunned, and grateful all at once as he let out a small laugh. "Let's go eat or whatever," she parroted back, and the two of them exchanged a knowing smile, which spoke louder than any words either of them could possibly conjure up.

Chapter Eleven

"Doctor Key," the nurse said in a tone that let him know it might be the hundredth time she'd said it even if it was the first time he'd heard it. "You need to call time of death; she's gone."

He was straddled across the body of a young woman who looked remarkably like his dead wife. His hands were locked into fists and pumping hard compressions on her chest. He knew he'd cracked a few ribs but they would heal if he could just get her damn heart beating again.

"No," he grunted, winded from the CPR workout. "I'm not stopping," he explained as sweat dripped off his brow and landed all over the woman's pale face.

"Dr. Key, she's been down for twenty-nine minutes. She's gone," another nurse said, placing one hand on his forearm that was still pumping up and down.

"Get off me," he hissed as he narrowed his eyes at the nurse, letting her know if she didn't there would be consequences.

The nurse compressing the bag that was breathing for the woman let go and took a step back. Her eyes were wet with tears that had dripped down on her surgical mask, soaking it.

"What are you doing?" Noah asked, his voice boiling with anger. "You have a responsibility. Pump that goddamn bag right now, or I'll make sure this is your last damn day as a nurse." When she shook her head somberly and folded her hands together he knew she was useless to him now. "Mary," he begged to the only nurse whose name he knew in the room. "Pump the damn bag, Mary. We have a responsibility. I took an oath."

"Do no harm," Mary whispered as she turned off the beeping machine that was showing a flat line where the woman's heart rate should be. "Dr. Key, she's gone."

"She's not gone. Rayanne," he said in a gravely grunt that sent every eye in the room turning toward him.

"This isn't Rayanne," Mary explained gingerly, but it only enraged him more.

"I know it's not," he yelled, still pumping on her chest fiercely. "I can see it's not her. I know."

The door to the triage room opened, and two of his fellow doctors entered. They had clearly been informed of the situation by someone who had left, looking for help.

"Noah," Martin Framer said, clearing the room with the wave of his hand. Everyone tiptoed out hurriedly, whispering as they went. Martin's bald head was shining under the florescent lights, and his glasses were pushed up on his forehead so he could look directly in Noah's eyes with no obstruction. "She's dead. Step down. Let her go."

The second doctor, Seth Tolpin, stepped forward and crouched his lanky body slightly so he was in Noah's line of sight. "We lose people Noah; you know that. It happens every day here. We can't save them all."

"Shut the hell up," Noah demanded. He looked down at the girl's lifeless face as it bounced slightly under the force of his compressions. "Don't lecture me. I have worked in this hospital for ten years. I've saved more lives than the two of you combined, and I've let more people go. Don't talk to me like I'm some intern."

"Then why are you still working on her?" Martin asked, folding his arms over his chest, seeming to lose patience with the situation.

"She deserves a chance. What kind of life has she had so far? She's wasted it. She deserves a chance to have a real life." He uttered the words manically as his arms began to cramp up.

"If we call security, Noah, your career will be significantly damaged. Get down now, let her go, and we'll keep this quiet. We'll say you were just exhausted, that the train accident had us all up for over twenty-four hours. Take a couple days off and rest. You can still get out of this." Seth was talking as though Noah was standing on the edge of a skyscraper about to jump, and it was his job to get him to reconsider. Something about that struck Noah. Was this career suicide? Could he live without this place? This was all he had left.

His arms froze, finally halting his compressions, and he took a breath. This woman was dead. No amount of CPR or other interventions would bring her back. If she had wasted her life with a man who gave her so little and kept her from her dreams then that couldn't be fixed now. Just like it couldn't be fixed for Rayanne. Everything he'd robbed his wife of could not be repaid.

Noah came down off the stretcher and dropped heavily into a chair in the corner of the room. His head rested in his hands, elbows propped on his knees. "Time of death," he murmured, "nine thirty-eight.

Chapter Twelve

"I'm going out for a smoke," Jamie said, spinning around his stool at the bar and hopping down. He slapped a pack of cigarettes against his palm a few times and then disappeared out the restaurant door.

"That guy really said that to you?" Travis asked, clinking his wedding ring against the glass in his hand. She had often wondered if there would come a day when she would stop wearing hers, but she couldn't imagine that. Seeing that Travis still had his on made her feel better about the prospect of keeping hers on as long as she wanted.

"I have a feeling he goes to grief groups a lot and preys on women. At first I was in such shock I couldn't even speak. You always assume you're going to respond forcefully at that moment, but I just froze. I couldn't believe what he was saying, what he was trying to do. By the time I was actually afraid, Jamie was there." She instinctively touched her neck where Paul had pressed his lips.

"I'm glad he was," Travis said, spinning around slightly to get a look at Jamie through the window. "Coming here today means a lot to him. I know it doesn't seem like much, but Jamie was trying to apologize to you today, and that's not something he does easily. If you'd have walked away it would have hurt him."

"I know." She nodded.

"Most people can't see it in him. They don't get that part of him. It's so easy to get caught up in what he's saying rather than understand why he's saying it. He wants me to be happy, and he thinks maybe you could make me happy, so he said something stupid. He didn't realize how you would feel."

"I just lost my husband," she breathed out, looking into her glass as though it were a crystal ball that could tell her future.

"I just lost my wife." Travis sighed. "It's been years, and it still feels like I just lost her. Autumn," he said, touching her arm gently, "whatever Jamie said, it's not what I'm looking for. You make him smile, and when he was running from me he ran to your house. That makes me want you around, but I'm not looking for more."

"Okay." She gulped back brewing tears and nodded her head. "I'm not sure why I make him smile though. I don't know why he'd run to my house. I don't have anything to offer."

"I don't know either," Travis admitted, looking like he regretted the frankness. "I just mean I'm not sure what he sees in you." He shook his head, angry with himself. "I don't mean that either."

"It's fine." She laughed. "Whatever it is, I'm glad if it helps him. I might be miserable, but it doesn't mean I want other people to be."

"I'm sorry you're miserable," he said, raising his glass and clinking it against hers as though they were toasting to unhappiness.

"Me too," she agreed, raising her glass of water and taking a sip. "Thanks for not telling me everything happens for a reason or how strong I am. Waking up and breathing does not make me strong. It's ridiculous. But at least tonight sealed the deal for me. I'm done with grief counseling."

"Really?" Travis asked, looking concerned. "I plan to call a couple buddies of mine on the force and report Paul. I don't think he'll show up there again."

"It's not Paul. I had decided about halfway through the meeting it would be the last one for me. Strangers aren't going to make this better. I want my husband back. They can't give me that."

"So what will get you through?" Travis asked, tilting his head slightly as he evaluated her face.

"What got you through?" she asked almost like she was accusing him of hypocrisy. He'd just agreed he was miserable.

"Jamie," he admitted. "I had someone else to worry about again, and that seemed to give me a reason to get out of bed. On days I didn't want to, I knew if I didn't he'd get in even more trouble."

She nodded her head. She could see how that would help a bit on the worst days. "Maybe I'll get a goldfish. Feeding it will keep me going," she joked sarcastically. Her phone chirped with a text message and sent her jumping. She had stopped returning the *'was just thinking of you'* text messages from her co-workers and friends. So over time they'd stopped sending them. Her phone had gone mostly silent the last month. She looked down at the screen and twisted her face in confusion.

"Everything all right?" Travis asked, reading her look of concern.

"Yes, I just got this strange text message. It says it's from *no sender.*" She started tapping her phone screen trying to investigate further. "It says, *I'm so sorry for the pain I caused.*"

"It doesn't say who sent it?" Travis asked, looking over her shoulder. "That Paul guy didn't have your number did he?"

"No, I didn't give it to him. Maybe he got my information through the group, but I don't think I gave it to anyone there. And why would it say no sender. That must be something someone has to do to block their number, right?"

"I guess so. You want me to have someone look into it for you?" Travis offered.

"No," she said, shaking her head and tucking her phone away. "It's probably just a wrong number or spam or something."

"If you get another one, let me know. I don't mind checking it out for you," Travis reiterated.

"Get another what?" Jamie asked, plopping back onto his stool as their food was being served. His musky smoky smell wafted toward Autumn, and she coughed.

"You stink," she said, waving away his smell.

"Not you too? Did he try to get you to tell me to quit smoking? Don't start," Jamie said, rolling his eyes and digging into the pile of fries in front of him.

"I don't care what you do," Autumn shot back. "I just don't want to smell you while you're doing it. Switch seats," she said, gesturing for Travis to come sit between them.

"Sure." Jamie smiled as though he knew something more was going on. He grabbed his plate of food and winked at Travis as they swapped barstools.

"You really do stink," Autumn defended. "I wasn't trying to get closer to Travis, just farther away from you. Don't start that crap again."

"I get it; you'll just keep me around to tackle guys like Paul. You didn't think I stunk then did you?" Jamie teased and leaned forward on the bar so he could raise his brows accusingly at her.

"Jamie—" Travis barked, his furrowed brows reprimanding him for talking like a jackass.

"Good point," Autumn cut in. "I guess I should cut you some slack at least for tonight. You've earned your French fries."

"Damn right," he laughed, shoving a handful into his mouth. "That guy was huge. He could have kicked my ass if he'd have gotten up."

"But you did it anyway," Autumn retorted.

"And I'd do it again," Jamie said through a full mouth. "He was a dickhead. Plus I knew Travis would be right behind me."

"You did?" Travis asked, crinkling his face as though he didn't believe him.

"Yeah, you told me to wait out front. I knew if I wasn't there you'd come looking for me right away. It's kind of your thing, chasing me."

"Lucky for you I guess." Travis laughed.

"The good thing about having you try to keep me in line is you're always watching my back. I figured between the two of us we could take the guy. I didn't really expect that right hook from you though."

"I used to box," Travis admitted bashfully. "I haven't hit someone in a really long time. It felt pretty good."

"Maybe I should try it," Autumn joked, mockingly cracking her knuckles as though she were preparing for a fight. She leaned over the bar and glanced at the two men as they dug into their plates of food. This wasn't completely awful. It wasn't too bad at all.

<u>Chapter Thirteen</u>

Noah rested his head despairingly on the steering wheel of his car. He'd been parked in his own driveway for three hours and couldn't seem to get out. He'd been home over the last few months, but this was different. He had nowhere else to run to. No distraction to hurry off to. He was on administrative leave for the next three days. He was not to step a single foot inside the hospital or even call in to check on a patient. This was his worst nightmare.

The moment he stepped into the house he knew the walls would come crashing in around him. If he immersed himself in the place that held all his yesterdays with Rayanne, it would be over. There would be no heading back to work because he'd have gone mad. He grabbed a bottle of pills from his pocket and quickly downed three of them. It was two too many, but he was desperate.

It's startling how you can miss what's going on around you when you let your dammed up emotions begin to flood you. That's likely why Noah didn't hear the car pull up behind him or the click of high heels against his driveway. It wasn't until a tap on his car window that he realized he was no longer alone.

"Noah," Donna said coolly as she peered at him through the car window. She was holding a large box in her hands and looked like she might drop it at any second. He released his painfully tight grip on the steering wheel and tried to tuck in all the loose pieces of his mind that had begun to unravel.

"I didn't expect you Donna," Noah said, stepping out of the car and taking the box from his mother-in-law's hands.

"Likewise," Donna retorted flatly. "I just assumed you'd be at the hospital, so I was going to leave these out on the porch for you."

"What are they?" he asked, trying to peer into the half opened box.

"They're Rayanne's journals. I don't feel right reading them. Honestly, I know if I keep them I will. You on the other hand will probably not have the same temptation."

Noah would have to be deaf, dumb, and blind not to take notice of the shift in Donna. She was furious with him. Her cutting insults were usually padded with smiles and ambiguity, but today's was a direct hit. A torpedo shot directly at him without an ounce of regret showing on her face. It was impossible to blame her. He'd done everything possible to push her away.

"I'm sure she wouldn't mind you reading them." Noah propped the box up on the hood of his car and made no move to head inside the house. If he went inside there was a chance Donna would follow him. Not only was the house in complete disarray, ripe to be judged by a woman like his mother-in-law, he was also just not in the mood for company.

"It's not right. Women use their journals to process things. They bare their souls in them with the promise that what they say won't be read out of context. As tempting as it is, I know reading her highest highs and lowest lows wouldn't bring me any peace." Donna stared at the box as though she might be changing her mind. She was saying all the right things, but letting these journals go wasn't going to be easy.

"I'll store them, and if you decide you want them they'll be here for you," Noah assured her. It was the deepest he could dig for kindness right now.

Donna grunted back something he didn't catch and moved toward her car. "Oh," she said, speaking over her shoulder, "I finally heard back from Autumn, the other survivor of the accident. She's not interested in speaking with me. She hung up on me."

Noah read between the lines. That rejection from Autumn had pushed Donna to this place she was now existing in. Every single hand she'd reached out had been slapped away. Her help wasn't needed, and to a woman like Donna that left her with no identity. She'd been super mom. She'd been a confidant to so many. A healer. A listener. She could console. What she couldn't do was nothing. Because if she was doing nothing she was, by default, nothing herself.

"What did she say?" Noah asked, knitting his brows together in concern.

"That she wanted to be left alone. She begged me to stop reaching out to her. But I heard the pain in her voice. I could tell she was hurting. There has to be more that can be done for her." Donna looked down at her nails. Noah could tell she was trying to distract herself and took note of her reaction. It seemed she realized how long it had been since she'd paid any attention to her hands. Gone were her weekly appointments for manicures and clearly she wasn't happy with the result.

"I'm sure she's doing the best she can. If she's trying to put the accident behind her then hearing from you was probably just too much. Don't take it personally," Noah explained. He was honestly trying to make her feel better but his choice of words had missed the mark. It was something that happened often in his life, but he'd never really worked to make it any better. He said the words that came to his mind. If someone took them the wrong way what could he do about it?

"Thanks for the advice," Donna laughed angrily as he continued to her car, not offering a goodbye.

Donna drove away, and Noah was alone again. If he slipped back into his car what would he do, just sit there for a few more hours? Grabbing the box, he moved to the porch and sank down onto the steps. His body was sore and, with the pills, his mind was sinking. He couldn't take much more of this.

Chapter Fourteen

Autumn stared at her phone and tried to fight the sensation of her throat closing up. The text message from the same mysterious sender read: *You shouldn't be alone. It shouldn't be this way.*

She'd promised Travis if she received another text she'd have him look into it, but something was stopping her. There was a vulnerable feeling encompassing her life without Charlie. She had to wonder, what made Travis trustworthy? What made him any different than Paul, the jerk from grief counseling?

The right thing to do would be to go right to the police and not depend on someone who essentially was still a stranger. She read the message again and thought who might be sending them. Paul was a real possibility. She wasn't sure how he'd have gotten her number, but it was the age of technology, surely it wouldn't be impossible to track her down. As a matter of fact she'd been tracked down pretty recently. Donna Ripper had found her address somehow and left her countless notes on her door. When Autumn shut her down maybe she decided these text messages would be another way to connect with her.

Could it be Jamie? He was standing outside when the first text came through. Though he seemed to like her well enough, he was still a troubled guy. And Travis. Seemingly a kind and harmless man, but what did she really know about him?

Charlie would tell her not to trust anyone just yet. He was a cautious man. Meticulously sensible and that had always served him so well. Slipping into her shoes, she grabbed her car keys off the hook they'd been planted on since the night of the accident and caught herself as though she'd physically just slipped. Her car had been in the driveway for months now. She'd resigned herself to never driving again, even though it was painfully inconvenient. Maybe this was a sign. She'd reached for her keys without a second thought. That must have meant something.

As the various key chains and store discount cards dangled in her hand, she gave it some serious consideration. All it took was closing her eyes for a moment and the flash of oncoming headlights made her drop them quickly. Dialing for a cab, she drew in a deep breath. She just wasn't ready. Not yet.

It would have taken her ten minutes to get to the police station if she'd jumped in her car and driven. But calling a cab had lost her about forty minutes.

With her phone clutched tight in her hand she pulled open the glass door to the precinct and stepped in, trying to look confident. It was quieter than she'd imagined. Too many cop drama shows gave her the impression this place would be littered with men in black ski caps and tattoos that had recently been slapped into handcuffs. Instead there was one older woman sitting on a bench, filling out some paperwork on a clipboard.

"May I help you?" an officer asked as he strolled up to her, his hands resting casually on the large belt at his waist.

"Um, I'm sorry," she said, the ever-present apology rolling off her tongue even when she wasn't sure what she was sorry for. "I have a question about some text messages I've been receiving. It's probably nothing."

"Do I know you?" the officer asked, raking his eyes over her face. "You look familiar to me."

"I don't think so," Autumn said confidently. She'd had very few run-ins with the law over the years. Not even a speeding ticket to her name. "I'm Autumn Chase."

"Oh, yes. The accident on highway forty? Was that you?" he asked with a light of recognition in his eyes.

The lump in her throat now grew three times larger. She wasn't expecting to have to talk about that at all today. She was going to ask a couple questions about these text messages and that was all. "Yes," she replied simply. Her eyes looked down at her shoes, instantly sending the message she'd rather not talk too much about it.

"I was one of the first responders," the officer said. "I'm Officer Pete Townsman. I'm so sorry for your loss. Why don't you come back to one of the private rooms with me, and we can talk about whatever you need." He gestured toward the back of the room, and she followed.

When they entered the tiny windowless room Autumn immediately regretted her choice to come. All she could think was she should have thanked Officer Townsman for helping her that night. She should have replied to his condolences. But the moment had passed.

"So Autumn, what's going on today?" he asked as he grabbed a clipboard and took a seat across from her.

"It's probably nothing," she said, feeling stupid now. "A few days ago I got a text message, and it just said *no sender,* and I got another one a little while ago."

"What do they say?" he asked, looking concerned. She passed her phone over to him and watched as he scrolled through and read the message. "Hmm," he hummed, the worry melting off his face.

"These aren't threatening or derogatory in any way. What about them would you like to report?" He handed the phone back and put his notebook and pen on the table, as though he wouldn't need them now.

"I don't know who sent them or why." Her cheeks burned with embarrassment as she realized how dumb all of this must sound.

"You haven't replied yet and asked who it was?" Officer Townsman shrugged. "You could start there. Technology can be pretty hokey. The fact that it says no sender could mean anything really. Is there any reason you feel this is something to be concerned about?"

"I had a run-in with a man at a grief group last week," Autumn choked out, feeling like she better add some meat to this complaint before she was laughed out of the place. "He

82

was very aggressive, and I was scared for my safety. The first text message came a few hours after that. I don't know how he would have acquired my phone number, but if it is him, I don't want to engage his text messages."

Those were the magic words. Townsman sat up a little straighter and cocked an eyebrow at her. "I heard about this," he said, grabbing his phone and scrolling through as though he was pulling something up. "Yeah, we have a cop here on the force that got a tip from one of his buddies about this. I didn't know it was you."

She felt her chest tighten as she thought of Travis. She'd promised him if she got another text she'd tell him, and now here she was sitting in the police station instead. It screamed, *I don't trust you.* But she had to remind herself how unimportant that was in the grand scheme of things. She didn't owe him her immediate trust.

"I didn't realize anyone had reported it. There were other people there from the group, and they must have done so. I should have reported it myself, but I just wanted to put it behind me." She raised her hand to where Paul's mouth had touched her neck and felt as though it was burning.

"I completely understand, Autumn. That's very common. I can tell you we've already followed up with this guy kind of off the record." He lowered his voice as he explained. "We just wanted him to know we were watching him since we didn't have an actual victim to make a statement. Now if you'd like to go on record about the incident we can make this more formal."

"I'm probably overreacting," she said with a nod, trying to convince herself.

"Actually," Townsman interrupted, "it's more common than you think for people to try to take advantage of a widow."

That word made her ears fill with static. She still couldn't believe she fit that title. It was for old women who outlived their husbands and rocked away in chairs on porches.

She shook the image away as Townsman continued, "People sometimes think there is a surge of money from life insurance, and they prey on the emotional distress. They'll insert themselves into your day-to-day and hope you begin to trust them. Some are more overtly intrusive like the encounter you had the other day. Both are unsettling, but I'd tend to be more worried about the people who play the long con. They're usually more dangerous."

Autumn's mind flashed to Jamie and then Travis. They were two new additions to her life who seemed to keep turning up out of the blue. "If I could just find out who was texting me it would put my mind at ease. Is there any way to see who these are coming from?" Autumn looked at her phone again and reread the text messages.

"Unfortunately we're a very small precinct here. We don't have a technology crime department. We outsource all of that, and this case wouldn't warrant it because there are no actual threats in the text messages. It's really up to you to decide how you want to proceed. We can put the screws to this Paul guy if you want to."

"What are my other options?" she asked, shifting uncomfortably in the rigid wooden chair.

"Well you can reply to the text and try to get more information from the person. You can ignore it and hope it doesn't escalate to something more. Or you can change your phone number." Townsman looked disappointed she wasn't leaning toward going on the record against Paul.

"I really don't want to start anything right now. It's been so hard lately for me without Charlie," she explained somberly. "I don't think I have it in me. I just want this to go away."

His face softened, and he nodded. "No problem. Please do me a favor and call if anything changes, or you feel like you're in danger." He pulled his business card from his shirt pocket and slid it across the table toward her.

"Thank you," she whispered, looking at the card and hoping she'd never have to call his number.

"I'll walk you out to your car," Townsman offered with a gentle smile.

"I don't drive," she sighed. "I'll take a cab home. That's how I got here. I haven't been able to get back behind the wheel yet."

"Autumn," he pulled open the door and gestured for her to step out of the small room first, "I've been on the force for over ten years, and your accident was the worst I've ever seen. It still keeps me up at night if I'm being honest. I can't imagine what it must be for you. Are you getting the help you need?"

That question was vague. What kind of help would actually make a difference at this point? Was there some kind of magic therapy session she could go to? "I'm just taking it one day at a time." That was a phrase she'd picked up a couple months back, and it silenced the endless questions from concerned people.

"That's all we can do really." He smiled and waved her off as she headed toward the front door. She hadn't really accomplished anything by coming here. She was no closer to knowing who sent the text messages. She lifted her phone to dial the cab company, and it chirped again. Another text message. But this time it wasn't a mysterious sender. It was Jamie.

Guess you aren't coming to this bullshit grief meeting tonight. Thanks for bailing on me. Buy me a cheeseburger, and we'll call it even.

She stood for a moment considering her reply. There was nothing to her lately. No content of any kind. Nothing she said was interesting. She'd given up on trying to look even halfway decent. Why would anyone be inviting her for a cheeseburger? *Interjecting into her life.*

She tapped the screen on her phone and fired back a message. *I'm not feeling well. I'll have to pass. Maybe next time.*

85

Dialing the cab company, she told herself she was doing the right thing. Now wasn't the time to make new friends. It wasn't the time to step on any ledges. Her bed was calling her name. The nest of covers and blackout curtains were all she needed.

Chapter Fifteen

Noah was a rock. The solid ground on which his wife could stand tall. He gladly owned the titles of problem solver and protector. But being a rock meant when thrust into the sea of despair he'd sink. He thought this pain was something he could endure and then eventually overcome.

Maybe he could outsmart it or distract himself from it, but up until this point nothing had worked. Nothing, that is, but the tiny bottle of pills rattling around in his pocket. When he took them he lost chunks of time and was probably sliding down a slippery slope. But they had the effect he needed. Numbing.

If he wouldn't be allowed at work, and he couldn't bear to be home, then he'd take the tiny pills along with a duffle bag full of his stuff and hide away. Checking into the hotel on the fringe of the city made him feel the best he'd felt in a long time. The room was neat and clean. The bed was comfortable and the shades could be drawn, making it impossible to tell if it was day or night.

The problem with being a doctor was sometimes you knew too much. He tipped the prescription bottle into his hand and watched the small oblong pills spill into his shaking palm. He knew the right concoction of these and a bottle of gin could put him out of his misery completely. It would quiet the guilt that circled his brain like bathwater being sucked down a drain.

Instead he plucked two from the pile and swigged them back with the bottle of hotel water he'd be charged nine dollars for. Closing his eyes, he flopped back onto the bed and let the medicine began to take effect. It could cloud him from his waking life, but sadly, the pills could not protect him from his dreams.

"Ray, why do you drag me to these things if you're just going to complain how I act when I'm here?" Noah hushed his voice as his wife dragged him down the hallway toward an

empty room. The house was nothing special, just cluttered with pictures of children and their artwork. He'd met Don and Sherry a handful of times, but he couldn't remember how many kids they had or how old they were. Don was a podiatrist who always wanted to talk shop as though Noah's job and his were one and the same.

"Maybe I hope when you get here you'll be able to act like a normal human being. I suppose that's too much to ask," Rayanne scolded, but Noah knew her voice well. Even as she came down hard on him the edges of her tone were playful. She knew as well as he did Don was a bit odd.

"It's New Year's Eve," Noah moaned and pulled his wife into his arms. "There are a million things we could do besides talking to Don and Sherry about their daughter's impressive spelling bee results in the semifinals. We've made the rounds, we've chatted, now can't we go?"

"It's ten thirty," Rayanne huffed. "We're staying until the ball drops. It's bad enough we aren't sleeping over. That's what everyone else is doing tonight. Sherry has the spare rooms all made up, and we're the only ones who aren't staying."

"Ray, you can blame that on me all you want, but I know you well enough. There is no way in hell you want to sleep here tonight. We're not twelve years old. We don't do slumber parties." He looped one of her curls around his finger and smiled in that way that always worked on her.

"Noah, you're impossible sometimes. Just be nice until the ball drops, and then we can go." She reached up and touched his cheek with her ice-cold hand. "Slow down on the scotch too, would you? That's your third one."

"If you were on your third glass of wine you wouldn't mind at all if I was getting a buzz. You'd think I was funny and charming. You've been milking that one glass for the last few hours. It's a terrible merlot isn't it? I knew we should have brought a bottle and not depended on Don to have something decent to drink."

"There's nothing wrong with the wine," Rayanne insisted as she sipped back some more and smiled. "Just please no more jokes about feet. Don's a podiatrist. We all get it. Go easy on the guy."

"Just be ready to kiss me at midnight," Noah swooned and leaned in to inhale his wife's familiar lavender perfume.

"Behave until then, and there's still a good chance I will." She planted a peck on his cheek and headed out of the small room, back to the party. As he moved to follow her, the floor beneath him shook. "Ray," he called, signaling for her to come back. "Don't go that way, Ray, come back."

The shaking grew stronger and the wooden floor beneath his feet split open. Ray looked back at him, crying out as the opening swallowed her up. "No Ray, don't go. Don't go where I can't go." As the abyss at his feet grew wider and deeper, he stared into it, contemplating what he should do. There was no hope of rescuing his wife. She would not have survived the fall.

A door behind him swung open, leading out to the warm fresh air of summer. He could see blooming flowers and smell the sweet scent of honeysuckle. He closed his eyes, spread his arms wide like the wings of a bird, and fell forward. Being with Rayanne was better than anything out that door.

A knock on the hotel door jolted him awake. He sprang off the bed and wiped at the cold sweat that had soaked his hair and forehead. The knock pounded again followed by an annoyed voice asking, "Turn down service?"

"No," he croaked out, his voice thick and his mouth dry. "No, thank you."

When the noise outside the door trailed off he felt as though he'd just fought off an intruder. He was relieved he wouldn't have to make small talk with a hotel housekeeper.

His hands were shaking as he flopped down onto the office chair in the corner of the room. He could feel his sweat sticking to the fake leather. "Noah," he said, punching his hand down on the desk, "for God's sake. What the hell am I doing?"

He glanced around the room for his phone, wondering if maybe someone from the hospital had called him. Perhaps they'd reconsidered sending him home, or someone was in desperate need of his medical advice. But his phone was nowhere to be found. He thought for sure he'd left it on the nightstand by the bed before dozing off. Who has he kidding, he hadn't dozed off; he'd medicated himself into a blackout coma.

Standing, he started throwing the covers off the bed and yanking up the pillows. He got down on his knees and looked around for his phone. Finally he picked up the hotel desk phone and dialed his own cell number. He heard his familiar ringtone chimes, but it sounded far off. Listening carefully, it seemed to be coming from the balcony. He hadn't been out there yet. He flipped the lock on the sliding glass door tentatively and stepped out into the warm air. There on the small glass table was his cell phone.

He lifted his phone from the table and inspected it closely. One missed call. It was from his attempt from the hotel room to find his cell. No one else had tried to contact him. The sun shone brightly onto his face, and he felt like he might melt under its cheeriness. Stepping back into the room, he closed the glass door. He yanked the curtains closed and brought darkness over the entire room. Grabbing the bottle of pills, he fished out two more, this time washing them down with a small bottle of vodka from the mini bar. Not bothering to fix the pillows or blankets, he collapsed on the bed and stared at the ceiling.

If he really did have the choice, would he jump into the same hole that had swallowed up his wife? Maybe that would solve everything.

Chapter Sixteen

Hunger really could be suppressed into oblivion if you were motivated enough. Autumn had lost her impulse to eat anything, and her bare cupboards had made hunger easier to live with. She had decided last night rather than sitting around being worried about the next text message she should just turn her phone off. If Mike needed to reach her to update her on his cancer treatment, he could call the house phone. There was no one else she needed or wanted to talk to.

It had been two days since her last text message from Jamie, asking her how she was feeling and why she kept blowing him off. But she let it go unanswered just like the three before that. There was no room in her cocoon for anyone else, and there was no way she was ready to break out of it. If the world were filled with people wanting to prey on her grief, why would she want to be out there? She needed no one.

As she walked toward the half bathroom she accidently caught a glimpse of herself in the hallway mirror. She looked as though she'd been transported back to the first few weeks after Charlie died. Again she wasn't eating, showering, or brushing her teeth. She'd regressed completely. And she didn't care. She'd removed all expectations from her life. And it all boiled down to this was what she really wanted.

Freezing in her tracks like a spooked animal she strained to hear what she thought was a knock on her door. She would just as soon crawl under her bed and hide than let someone in her house. It wasn't how she looked; it was how she felt. But the knocking continued. It grew louder and louder and then suddenly stopped. She used the reprieve to shuffle silently toward her room. The bathroom could wait.

But she wasn't safe there either. The tapping on her window reminded her of the first night Jamie had woken her in his drunken stupor. But this time it wasn't him.

"Autumn, are you okay?" Travis asked, tapping on the window again. "I'm not trying to bother you, but I'm worried. Just give me a sign of life, so I don't have to have the cops come do a welfare check."

"Travis, I'm fine. Thank you for coming by, but I just want to be alone." She let the anger show through in her voice.

"Thank God." Travis sighed, and she could hear the relief pouring from him. "Can you let me in for a minute? I just want to talk to you."

"I-I . . . it's just . . . I don't want to," she admitted. "I'm fine. I just don't want any company, that's all." She tried to think of a scenario where he would leave now, but none came to mind. He was dug in, and she was trapped.

"I don't plan to stay for a cup of coffee, Autumn. I've been where you are right now. I just want to talk to you for a minute. You aren't alone."

That was probably said to be comforting but, in her current state of mind, it was more of a threat than anything. *She wanted to be alone.*

"If you want me to go away, the quickest way is to just talk to me for a minute. That's not a bad trade-off, right?" Travis was trying to sound upbeat, but she could tell he was concerned.

"I'll meet you at the door," she acquiesced, solely for the purpose of getting rid of him quickly and not having to deal with the police knocking on her door, worried about her.

She didn't bother cleaning herself up. She was in dirty mismatched pajamas with the buttons aligned wrong. Her hair was in a knot at the top of her head. Her eyes were bloodshot and stinging from an overdose of tears. She tucked her feet into her slippers and shuffled toward her door. Pulling it open she stood stone-faced, staring back at Travis.

"Oh, Autumn," he said, his face crumpling in a mix of disappointment and worry. "Why didn't you call me? Why didn't you tell me you were struggling?"

"Why wouldn't I be struggling?" She shrugged. "I want to be alone. Please don't make me have to beg you to go."

"I don't want you to beg me, Autumn. I know being alone feels good right now, but it's not healthy. Are you eating? Have you slept?"

"Not really, and no," she admitted. "But I'm dealing with this. I'm having a rough patch." She lied, knowing she'd already resigned herself to this being her life now.

"Where is your cell phone? It's been going right to voicemail." He furrowed his brow in concern.

She leaned back into the house and reached for the table by the door where Charlie always put his keys when he got home from work. "I've had it off," she said, showing him the blank screen. She clicked the power button and watched it spring to life with chirps and beeps that indicated text messages. She scrutinized the screen.

"Jamie has been texting you, and he said he hasn't gotten an answer. He was worried," Travis said quietly, adding, "I was worried too."

"I wanted to unplug for a while," she explained, tucking the phone into her pajama pocket.

"Do you have food here? I can go grab whatever you want, if you make me a list. Even if you don't want to see me I can leave it at the door." Travis looked desperate to help now, not wanting to leave her without doing something.

She shook her head, ready to tell him she didn't need the food. A white flapping piece of paper caught her eye before she could speak. It was taped to her door and fluttering in the spring breeze. "Did you leave this?" she asked, pointing to the note accusingly.

"No," he insisted, shaking his head adamantly.

She yanked the taped note from her front door and unfolded it. *Autumn, I know that you are hurting. Please don't shut me out. Call me. Donna Ripper.*

Autumn crumpled the note in her fist and shook with anger. "Is she fucking kidding me?" she asked in a hiss.

"Who?" Travis asked, leaning to catch Autumn's wild eyes, since it seemed as though she was looking right through him.

"This woman. These people," she stammered, her mind clouding over, confusing things that were once very clear. "This dead girl's mother keeps stalking me. I told her to leave me alone, but she just won't stop. All these notes. She's probably sending the text messages too. You people. Can't you people leave me alone?" Autumn shouted, taking the crumpled note and slamming it into Travis's chest, trying to shove him backward.

"Autumn, who is stalking you? You're still getting the text messages?" Travis asked, holding the hand that had hit his chest.

"Let me go," she cried out, yanking her arm away. "You, you're probably sending the text messages. What do you want from me? You want Charlie's money? You think I'm a rich widow now or something? Maybe you want to scare me with the messages, so I go running right into your arms. Get away from my house." Autumn pointed over his shoulder fiercely. "Go away. Get away from me now."

"Autumn, please calm down. I think you're confused, and you're not thinking straight. You might be dehydrated or sleep deprived. That can wreak havoc on you. Why don't you sit down, and I'll get you a drink and something to eat. Just take a breath."

"Get out," she chanted. "Get away from my house."

Out of options, he let a look of resignation wash over him as he stumbled backward toward his car. "Autumn, just take a deep breath and try to calm down."

She lifted the pot that had once held a beautiful geranium and hurled it toward him. "Go," she shouted again as the pot smashed onto the driveway. Travis looked up at her in astonishment before hopping in his car and backing quickly out of the driveway.

Autumn looked down at the crumpled note by her feet and lifted one dirty slipper to stomp on it as though it were in flames. Stumbling backward, she slammed her front door and ran in a full sprint upstairs. Kicking off her slippers, she leaped into the bed and pulled the covers up like a child hiding from a monster in her closet.

"Leave me alone," she whispered, but her words were sliced in half by the chirp of her phone in her pocket. She'd forgotten to turn it off. Fishing it out, she let the light glow below the blanket she was hiding under. The screen said: nine text messages. Five were from Jamie. But four were from the mysterious blocked number. She wasn't sure when they'd come in, but she read them with a shiver up her spine.

This is too much.

I don't know where I am anymore. This has to end.

How do you go on? This doesn't work.

I'm so sorry. Forgive me. I don't see an answer.

Her anger and confusion turned from a simmer to a boiling rage, and she threw the phone with all her force against the wall. She wished it had shattered into a million pieces, but instead it just thumped to the floor. Yanking the covers back up over her head, she sobbed with such fury her muscles ached from the intensity. She just wanted all of this to end. If this were a nightmare, now would be the time to wake up.

Chapter Seventeen

Like a petulant child, Autumn plugged her ears with her fingers and pressed her eyes closed tightly. "Charlie, why did you do this to me?" she cried out. "How could you leave me alone?"

She kicked her feet against the mattress and pulled all the blankets from the bed. This was a temper tantrum, and it was the only relief she could find right now.

Suddenly, like a whisper in her ear, she thought she heard her husband's voice. "Charlie?" she asked, going stiff as a board. But the noise was gone. Rather than beginning her flailing again she just rolled to her side, clutched a pillow over her heart, and tried to remember a day she didn't hurt like this. A day she was happy.

The beach. That was the first thing that had come to her mind. She and Charlie didn't take nearly as many vacations as they should have. Surely if they knew he'd be dead by thirty-five, they'd have spent every second traveling. But one trip still stood out in her mind. Their long weekend in the Hamptons had been the perfect getaway. They didn't hit a single tourist attraction. Instead they spent every second tucked away on a little patch of land that came with the house they'd rented. It was this unique combination of woods and beach that made her feel like they were on some secluded island.

Every morning they'd walk the sand and never see another soul. After lunch they'd grab their floats and hold hands as they drifted in the calm afternoon low tide. They mixed drinks and watched old movies. Time had stood still long enough for them to be able to truly articulate and understand why they loved each other. It had been the happy place her mind always went back to when Charlie frustrated her with some day-to-day thing.

"Remember the Hamptons, Charlie?" She breathed out as she squeezed the pillow tighter. "We laughed so much. For hours we just held each other. That was the best time in my life, and it's already gone by."

"Autumn," a voice echoed up her hallway, and she felt a tingling heat prickle its way up her body. Who the hell had gotten in her house, and how? She thought for a second she was being robbed, but then considered the unlikely coincidence that they'd know her name. Before she could pull back her covers the voice was in her room.

"Autumn, it's Jamie," he said in his gravely and annoyed voice. "What the hell's going on? I had to talk Travis out of calling the cops to have them come check on you. He thinks you've lost it."

She flipped back the covers, shot to a sitting position, and tried unsuccessfully to get some of the static out of her hair. "How the hell did you get in my house?"

"Shit," Jamie spit out, stumbling back a bit at the sight of her. "What the hell happened to you? You look like something out of a horror movie. Did you really throw a pot at Travis?"

"How the hell did you get in my house?" she repeated through gritted teeth like a snarling tiger.

"I figured you'd have a spare key out there somewhere. No surprise it was under the first loose brick in the flowerbed wall. You should move it somewhere else." Jamie flashed the key at her and then placed in on the dresser next to him.

"Get out," she insisted, pointing at the door. "I will call the police."

"The only reason I'm here is so the police don't show up. Once they see you they'll call an ambulance, and you'll be hauled off to the funny farm. Trust me; that's no joke. You need to get your shit together and come downstairs. I brought you some soup. Eat that, maybe take a couple sleeping pills, and try to get rid of whatever is going on."

"Whatever is going on? My husband is dead." She slapped the pillow next to her as though she wished it were Jamie's face.

"He was dead last week, and you were fine. I was with you, so that's not it. What happened between then and now that's got you unraveling?"

"You are an insensitive callous jerk. Why are you here Jamie?" she snapped. "Maybe that's why I'm losing it. Why in the world are you here?"

"I just told you, take it from me, you don't want to end up strapped to a bed in the psych ward." He raised an eyebrow as though he were trying to compel her to take his advice.

"No Jamie, I mean why did you talk to me that night on the porch? Why did you come knocking on my door that night you were drunk? As far as I can tell you don't give a shit about anyone but yourself, so explain to me why you keep showing up in my life." Autumn's head was swiveling on her shoulders as she spat the accusations his way.

"What the hell happened to you? We were splitting a basket of fries last week, and this week you're acting like I'm some axe murderer. What changed?" Jamie met her raised voice and let his flailing arms display his anger. He wasn't backing down and showed no signs of leaving.

"I got some good advice from a police officer when I went to report these damn text messages." She gestured to her phone on the floor. "He told me that people can take advantage of women in my situation and start to integrate themselves into my life. Sound familiar?" She was manic in her explanation, but she didn't know how to lasso her words and get them to obey her.

"What text messages?" Jamie asked, homing in on the one piece of her rant that seemed important.

"Ha," she coughed out. "It seems somebody has my phone number and thinks that sending me bizarre text messages about pain and apologies is funny. And I can't be sure it isn't you or Travis, for that matter. And the cops aren't going to find out for me. So instead I'm just trying to stay the hell away from you guys, and men like Paul, and the crazy woman who keeps leaving notes on my door. So get out of my house, and I can go back to not being around you."

"Whoa," Jamie exhaled, running a hand through his hair as though he had to push the information she was giving him into his brain. "When did the text messages start?"

"The night I met Paul, so maybe it's him." She fell backward onto her pillow, staring up at the ceiling. It had felt good to yell, whether or not Jamie deserved it. But it had also wiped out her tired body.

"And who's the lady leaving the notes on your door?" Jamie asked, taking a few steps forward and cautiously deciding to sit on the foot of the bed.

"The woman who died in the accident that also killed my husband, it's her mother. Donna Ripper. She wants to talk to me, and I have nothing to say to her. I called her up and told her, but today there was another note from her. I can't deal with it, Jamie. I can't." Autumn covered her eyes with her hands, trying to block out any light.

"Yeah, I can imagine that must suck. But I'm not sending you any text messages, and I'm not integrating myself into your life, or whatever." He pulled at a loose seam on the quilt and fidgeted uncomfortably. "You asked why I talked to you that night and why I came here, it's because you remind me of my mother."

"Oh, go to hell," Autumn shot back angrily. "I'm like twelve years older than you or something."

"No, I'm not saying you could be my mother. I'm saying you remind me of my mother when she was young. I saw you in that meeting, and it was too heavy for me. The way you spun your ring on your finger and shook your leg like you were about to jump out of your skin, it was just how she used to be. Your eyes are exactly like hers."

Autumn had shimmied herself to a half sitting/half lying position and stared at him skeptically. "We have the same eyes? You mean bloodshot and red-rimmed from crying? Dark circles around them from no sleep?" She was being sarcastic and argumentative, but when she caught a flash of something in Jamie's eyes it silenced her.

"Exactly like that," Jamie replied. "I knew that night, when I was trying to dodge Travis that you'd let me in. I could just tell."

"Well, I wouldn't have today," she explained. "So it's a good thing you decided to break in, otherwise I'd still be angry at you."

"Are you not anymore?" Jamie asked hopefully.

"I'm too tired to be angry. I'm too exhausted to be anything right now."

"Travis is really worried," Jamie insisted. "He's about to call the funny farm for you, and I begged him not to. I brought some soup. If you eat and get some rest, maybe even shower, I know you can convince him you're all right."

"I'm not all right, Jamie." Autumn sighed.

"But you will be. And going to some rubber room won't speed that process up. Just eat, sleep, and shower, and you'll be fine."

"And should I move to another house so this woman stops trying to contact me? Should I get rid of my phone so whoever is sending the text messages leaves me alone? It's too much." She lay down, grabbing either side of the pillow and pulling it up so the fluffy down clogged her ears. When Jamie touched her leg gently she let go of the pillow to hear what he had to say.

"I'll take care of that stuff. You don't have to worry about it again. Just keep your phone off for now, and do the basic things that keep you alive. The other stuff I've got under control." Jamie's face was level and for the first time not full of attitude or sarcasm. This was genuine.

"What are you going to do?" she asked, worried he might not be the most tactful person to ward off someone causing her problems. But then maybe tact wasn't needed to really get the job done.

"That's you worrying about it." He raised an eyebrow at her accusingly. "Travis is going to want to come by and check on you tonight. He won't believe I was capable of making you feel better, and he wasn't."

"I threw a pot at him," Autumn whispered as she covered her face with her hands. "I launched a pot with a dead plant at him and screamed for him to leave me alone."

"You're probably dehydrated and sleep deprived. It can make you do crazy things. But take it from me; Travis is a pro at second chances. I think I'm on my fiftieth chance right now. I've done a lot worse than throw a pot at him. My things involve pot, but a different kind." Jamie laughed, and Autumn rolled her eyes.

"Why do you do all those things, Jamie? If Travis keeps giving you chances to change, why don't you?" She sat up and shimmied ungracefully to the side of the bed, standing uneasily. Jamie jumped to his feet and steadied her.

"You're a good person, Autumn, for thinking I'm not too far gone. No one would agree with you, but I still appreciate it."

"Charlie used to tell me anyone could change if you gave them a chance. He was a defense attorney, and he was one of the few who did the job because he actually believed in rehabilitation and real justice." She stared off as she spoke, remembering what it felt like to watch Charlie in the courtroom.

"That's a nice way to think I guess," Jamie offered, but she could tell he didn't agree with the logic, and frankly neither did she.

"He was wrong," Autumn announced, surprising Jamie with her candor. "He got burned so many times by people he stuck his neck out for. He'd fight to get them some sort of help, and they'd blow it off or ruin it. But he always kept trying."

"He sounds like a good guy," Jamie replied, stuffing his hands in his pockets and heading for the bedroom door.

"He is," she smiled before her memory kicked in, shattering her face. "He was."

<u>Chapter Eighteen</u>

Noah straightened his tie and ran his fingers through his hair to tamp it into place. The hotel was trashed, littered with garbage and cigarette butts. It was a no smoking room, and he'd be charged a fortune in cleaning expenses, but he didn't care. The only thing that mattered was getting back to work. Whatever the last three days were, they were now over.

All he needed to do was snap on a pair of gloves and save someone's life. It would recharge every weak part of him. He grabbed his duffle bag and headed out, the sunlight stinging his eyes. This was the first time he'd stepped out of the hotel room since he checked in, and he felt like his body was struggling to acclimate with the fresh air and outside noise. It would all be all right the second he got back to work.

He grabbed a coffee to perk himself up, and by the time he was standing in front of the glass doors of the emergency room he felt like a million bucks. That lasted roughly thirty seconds because the moment he saw the chief of staff standing at the nurses station he knew something was up.

"Noah, I've been waiting for you," Clark Masterly said with a smile and extended hand to greet him.

"Clark, how's everything?" he asked, trying to read the subtle signs on Clark's pasty wrinkled face.

"Good, good," Clark said with a nod. "Can I get a few minutes with you in my office?" He gestured for Noah to lead the way, but he didn't budge.

"I've got to start rounds," Noah retorted, planting his shiny dress shoes to the waxy linoleum floor.

"Dr. Sparks has you covered this morning. No need to worry." Clark gestured again for Noah to head down the hallway.

"No, he's been covering my patients for the last few days, but today I'm back, and I need to see how badly he's screwed them up." Noah smirked but Clark did not.

"Noah, please come into my office. We need to talk, and I don't want to do this on the floor." Clark leaned in close as he whispered, and Noah fought the urge to smack him away.

"No Clark, if you have something to say please by all means, speak freely." Noah raised his arms and gestured around the room as though he didn't care who heard him.

"Let's not make *another* scene. Come on into my office, and we can talk about this rationally." Clark's overgrown brows furrowed in anger.

"Another scene, oh I see you are trying to make something out of what happened in the triage room. It was nothing. I'm fine and ready to be back at work. Whatever bureaucratic red tape you want me to jump through, you can have me do it after my shift. Nothing is keeping me from rounds this morning."

"You're suspended indefinitely," Clark snapped back. "Security will be happy to keep you from your patients if it comes to that. But I hope it won't. Now if you come into my office we can discuss options."

"What kind of options?" Noah scoffed.

"Separation options. Trust me, you want to really consider how you respond in the next half hour. Don't burn this bridge, Noah. We understand you've been through a lot in the last few months, but that doesn't mean we can put the liability on the hospital. Now, we have every intention of compensating you in a manner you deserve and not exploring any deeper into some of the issues that have arisen. That's going to depend on how you handle yourself right now."

This was not the chest-puffing ego move Clark usually laid on everyone to compensate for being the shortest guy in every room. Noah could see it now. This was no pissing match. It was his career hanging in the balance. Without another word he clenched his jaw tightly and marched toward Clark's stuffy office.

The door closed behind them, and Clark took a seat in his plush leather chair. Noah waved off the offer for him to take the seat across from him. "I'll stand," he grunted.

"Noah, some things have been brought to my attention I cannot ignore. You and I have worked together for over five years, and while I know you to be a very competent doctor, I've always had my concerns about your bedside manner and your basic compassion for people."

"Excuse me?" Noah asked, his voice laced with indignation.

"You tend to be cold and aloof. You've never attended any events for the hospital or socialized with any of your colleagues. The tendency on your part is to treat your patients like a challenge rather than like people. I've seen you save a lot of lives Noah, but I've seen you hurt a lot of people as well."

"I was doing CPR," Noah defended. "Maybe I should have called it earlier, but I wanted to give the girl a fighting chance."

"It's not that, Noah," Clark continued, raising his hand up to silence him. "These were issues we had with you before your tragic loss, and I'm afraid they've been made worse. They are now at a level that puts patients and other staff members in uncomfortable and maybe dangerous situations. Especially because I believe it might be fueled or amplified by a dependence and abuse of prescription drugs."

"Go to hell," Noah barked back.

"Multiple staff members reported getting frantic and ranting phone calls from you over the last few days. They were made to feel very uncomfortable, and some were even worried for their safety. You've written yourself multiple prescriptions over the last few months. How you managed it, I'm not sure. Now I encourage you to take this time off to seek treatment and counseling so you may one day practice medicine again. Against my better judgment, and because I know how hard of a loss you've suffered, I've decided not to report my concerns, in the hope that you will come through this. Until further notice, you are suspended indefinitely. We can reevaluate your status in thirty days." Clark leaned back in his chair and folded his arms across his chest.

"So, I'm not the guy at every hospital cookout, wearing a funny apron and a goofy pair of shorts. That means I'm not a good doctor? The pills I've been taking have been to manage my anxiety after the loss of my wife. I have not abused or overused them, nor have I let them interfere with my work. I didn't make any phone calls to anyone on staff in the last few days," Noah asserted, but there was a nagging voice in the back of his head that wasn't sure if that was true. "Do your damn research before you make a decision like this."

"We did Noah." Clark stood and gestured toward the door. "Keep in touch with me. Please reach out if you need any sort of assistance. This might seem like we're hurting you, but in the end we may be saving your career." Clark rounded his desk and opened the door when Noah seemed to be standing like a stubborn mule.

"Whatever," Noah growled as he headed for the door. What Clark didn't know was this job was the very thin thread holding Noah's seams together. Now that it had been snipped, he would burst apart into confetti, never to be repaired.

Chapter Nineteen

Hot. It was a sensation Autumn could still measure even when her heart felt stone-cold. The blazing heat of the shower. The steaming soup that burned its way down her throat. Even the clean clothes she'd pulled from the dryer with the burning hot metal button of her jeans. She hadn't wanted to believe a long nap, some food, and cleaning herself up would actually make her feel a little better, but it had. Not nearly healed, but at least her brain wasn't as foggy.

Her hair was still sopping wet so she spun it up into a towel and dabbed a little makeup on her face. It seemed a silly thing to do this late in the afternoon, but she knew Travis would be by soon, and she didn't want him to think she was ready for the nut house. Proving that would be an uphill battle, considering how she acted that morning.

When the doorbell rang she drew in a deep breath, stared hard into her own eyes in the mirror, and forced composure on her face.

"Hi," she said quietly as she welcomed Travis in. "Thanks for coming back. I really wanted a chance to apologize for earlier."

"It's me who should apologize," Travis interrupted. "I just wanted to help, but I should know by now trying to force someone to do anything when they're hurting is a bad idea. All this time with Jamie has taught me nothing, I guess."

"It's taught him a few things if that counts," Autumn said as she grabbed two mugs from her cabinet and poured some fresh coffee. She remembered how he took his and readied it for him.

"What do you mean?" Travis asked, looking skeptical of the compliment.

"He was helpful when he was here. I think he's likely learned a lot of that from you. I wasn't expecting to be up and walking around right now, and he had a lot to do with that."

She slid the mug across the kitchen island and gestured for him to sit down.

He looked too stunned to move. "I'll be honest when Jamie said not to call the police to come check on you, I wasn't sure what he was angling at. I never thought you'd open the door for him."

She laughed into her mug. "I didn't. He let himself in and came right up to my room. We were pretty much screaming at each other for a little while, but then he said something that gave me a glimpse into him."

"And what was that?" Travis asked, stirring his coffee and tilting his head as though he couldn't wait for the answer.

"He told me I reminded him of his mother. And if that's really true, the state I've been in since he met me tells me a lot about how his mother must be. Or how she was. Is she not alive anymore?" Autumn wasn't intentionally prying; she just couldn't imagine a woman in her current condition raising a child. And part of her wanted to know what became of women like her.

"Like I said before, it's not my story to tell. My relationship with Jamie is already fragile enough. If he knew I shared something with you he wanted to keep private, it could be the end. I hope you understand."

"Of course," she assured him. "I was just wondering. Don't break his confidence. But I did think you should know he really was persuasive, and though it wasn't the kindest approach, it worked. He has a unique way of being effective."

"Good," Travis said, but Autumn could tell he still didn't look convinced. "You do seem like you're doing a lot better."

"I'm not throwing any pots, if that's what you mean." She smiled. "It was a combination of a few things that put me in that state. I went to the police station to report those text messages, and the officer warned me about new people popping up in my life. I got spooked about your intentions. I felt like I'd never know how to trust anyone again. When I started losing more than a little sleep and didn't eat much of anything, I guess it caught up with me. Plus I had that woman leaving messages on my door. It was too much."

"I'm sorry you felt like you couldn't trust me or that I was around for the wrong reasons. There's really nothing I can say to convince you otherwise, but if you let me stick around long enough, hopefully I'll find a way to prove it. All of the other stuff, the notes and the text messages, are something we can look into more. If it's making you uncomfortable, then we can find a solution."

"Jamie said he'd work it out," Autumn explained and topped off his coffee. "I think that's the main thing that got me out of bed. Just hearing someone say it would all go away made me feel like I could keep going."

Travis didn't make a move for the refilled mug. "What do you mean, Jamie said he'd work it out? Work what out?" There was a sudden stiffness in his back that sent shivers up her spine.

"I don't know." She shrugged, feeling defensive. "I told him about the notes on the door and the text messages that started the night the thing happened with Paul, and he said he'd handle it. I wouldn't have to worry about any of it anymore."

"Shit," Travis grunted as he banged his hand down on the counter. "By what means did you think he'd be handling this stuff? You can't ask a kid like Jamie to do that. He's not going to be able to say no, and in the process he's going to get himself into a lot of trouble. He's on probation. I've worked for a very long time to keep him out of jail, and that's all down the tubes now."

"Wait a second," Autumn interrupted, hopping to her feet. "I didn't ask him to do anything. He offered. How is that going to get him thrown in jail?"

"You remind him of his mother. He sees you hurting and needing help, of course he's going to do whatever it takes to make you feel better. Jesus, Autumn, you should have known better. What did you think he was going to do to solve these problems?"

"How should I know? If I knew that answer I'd have done it myself and been finished with it by now." She watched as Travis moved frantically through the house, pacing as he dialed his cell. "Jamie, call me back the second you get this message. It's urgent." He hung up quickly and ran his hands over his anxious brows. "I need you to tell me exactly what he knows."

"I, um," Autumn tried to understand what was happening as she recalled her conversation with Jamie. "I told him the mother of the woman killed in the accident that night had been leaving notes on my door. I tried to tell her I wasn't interested in talking to her, but she was still doing it."

"Did you tell him her name?" Travis clarified, a bite in his voice.

"I think so, yes." Autumn covered her hand with her heart as Travis's uneasiness filled the room around her.

"What else?" he demanded.

"I just told him about the text messages."

"And he assumes they are from that jackass, Paul?"

"I guess so." She sighed. "I mean if they aren't from you, and they aren't from Jamie, Paul is the only other person I can think of that's popped into my life and might have a reason to send me strange messages."

"I've got to go," Travis announced, fishing his keys from his pocket and lunging for the front door.

"Wait a second, where are you going? What am I missing?" She clutched the sleeve of his shirt and stared up at him desperately.

"Jamie knows one form of conflict resolution. He blows it up. This woman leaving notes at your door and Paul are about to come face to face with a kid who thinks the best way to solve a problem is to destroy everything he touches."

"But Paul's a lot bigger than Jamie, he's not going to go there and get physical with him, right? That doesn't make sense."

"Jamie won't be unprepared this time. If he's going over there to set this guy straight about bothering you, he'll have something planned. Something that will land him in jail. I have to stop him." Travis shook off her hand and opened the door.

"If he thinks this is what I want him to do, it won't matter what you say, will it? He needs to hear it from me."

Travis froze, clearly mulling over her logic. "Right," he nodded. "But I can't guarantee what you'll see. I don't know exactly what he'll have planned. It'll certainly change the way you think of him."

"That's not important. I just want to stop him." She spun the towel off her head and let her hair fall all around her face in a mess. As she hopped into the passenger seat of the car, she clicked her seatbelt and centered herself with a deep breath. "How does he even know where to find them?" she asked, wondering if Travis might be overreacting.

"Jamie might not show it, but he's brilliant. He can do anything with a computer. Through some court-ordered stuff he's been tested, and his IQ is off the charts. Why do you think he has that flashy car but no job? He can turn a little money into a whole lot by using his brain. It's dangerous for a guy like him."

"It would take him time to track them down. He only has Paul's first name."

Travis hung his head as he thought through his mistakes. "I called my buddies at the precinct about Paul. I knew you didn't want to make a formal complaint, but I still wanted answers. With the statement I provided they were able to track him down. They gave me all his information too, and I wrote it down near my computer. I'm sure Jamie knew it was there. I think I told him about it. As far as the other woman, he'll find her the same way she found you. Public records and the Internet."

"And what's he going to do to a mourning mother who probably didn't mean any harm?" Autumn asked, thinking of the poor woman who'd already been through enough.

"I have no clue," he admitted. He pulled out his phone and clicked away at the screen. "Here, I have a GPS on Jamie's car he doesn't know about. Pull it up and let me know where he is right now."

Autumn fiddled with the app and found the location. "He's about fifteen minutes from here on the corner of Elk and Midway." Clicking in the directions, she passed the phone back and let Travis take a look.

"That's not Paul's house," he explained, zooming in to try to make sense of Jamie's location.

"Do you think he went to the woman's house first?" Autumn asked with a gasp. She searched her phone frantically, scouring the Internet for Donna Ripper's address. "He did," she confirmed, feeling her stomach loop into knots.

"I hope you're good at damage control," Travis said as he shoved his foot down on the accelerator. Autumn's body was forced backward against the seat.

"What have I done?" she whispered and closed her eyes. "What the hell have I done?"

Chapter Twenty

Noah stared at the box he'd just slammed onto the kitchen table and realized it wasn't the only one. Not only was there a box of his belongings from his locker at work, there was also the box Donna had left for him. It was full of journals his wife had kept for as long as he had known her and probably many years before. He'd never even cracked one open. Other men, self-conscious or jealous ones, probably would have snooped, but it had never crossed his mind to invade his wife's privacy. He never had to. Rayanne was an articulate woman and never hesitated to tell him how she was feeling. Even when he was only pretending to listen to her.

But maybe he was wrong. Maybe there were thousands of things in those journals he never knew about her. And what if they shattered his idea of who his wife really was and how she felt about him?

Reading them would likely bring him nothing but questions that could never be answered. He forced the flaps of the box in on each other and slid the box off the table and onto the floor. Grabbing a glass and a bottle of Scotch, he flopped into the kitchen chair and fished a few more pills out of his pocket. He couldn't believe they thought he was a drug addict. Well if he couldn't convince them they were wrong, then maybe he should just prove them right.

<u>**Chapter Twenty-One**</u>

"He's not here," Autumn said, her voice laced with worry as she craned her neck and searched for his car. The house they'd pulled in front of looked like it was straight out of a storybook. The shutters matched the trim. The flower boxes were overflowing with wispy, romantic blooms. The lawn was precisely groomed. The cars in the driveway looked freshly waxed. There was no sign of a Jamie tornado blowing through.

But Autumn knew better than to trust the outward appearance of anything. Even she could clean herself up and dust herself off enough to look like she was doing just fine.

"There's a bit of delay on the GPS. But he was parked right here. We should go check things out and make sure everything is all right." Travis put the car in park and unfastened his seat belt. He gripped the steering wheel tightly and seemed to silently will himself to get out of the car. "You can stay here if you want. I know the whole point of this was to avoid having to deal with this woman, and here you are at her house."

"No, I should be there. Whatever he's done, it's on me." She pushed her shoulder into the car door and swung it open.

"I'm sorry I said that." Travis sighed and rounded the car, meeting her stride toward the quiet house. "You had no way of knowing how he operates."

Neither one of them knocked when they reached the door. Instead they just stared at each other for a moment as though they were going to jump out of a plane in tandem. Finally Travis raised his arm and rapped on the door. A few seconds later a round-faced woman opened it. Autumn's heart sank as she took in the wetness in the woman's eyes.

"It's a day for strangers at my door," she said, forcing a smile.

"Jamie?" Travis asked, not looking capable of forming a complete sentence.

"Yes," she answered skeptically.

"I'm very sorry to show up here today," Autumn apologized. "And Jamie—I want you to know that he means well."

"Who are you exactly?" Donna asked, looking back and forth between them.

"I'm Travis, and this is Autumn—" he began, but she cut in.

"Autumn Chase," she said, watching Donna's face to see if there was a reaction. And it wasn't subtle by any means.

"Oh, considering the conversation I had with young Jamie I didn't really expect to be seeing you."

"I didn't have any intention of coming," Autumn admitted. "But once I knew Jamie had been here, I felt like I better come explain."

"He did a fairly good job of it," Donna said as she cleared her throat, sounding uncomfortable.

"Jamie's a good kid," Travis started, and Autumn imagined this speech had been given to many people over the years.

"Obviously," Donna agreed, and neither of them knew her well enough to distinguish if this was sarcasm. Instead they just waited to hear more. "I really do apologize for hounding you so much Autumn. Jamie explained to me what you've been dealing with, and I didn't mean to contribute to that stress. I'll tell you what I told him if you'd like to come in and talk. He had a cup of coffee and some cookies with me, but there are plenty of both left."

"He sat with you and had cookies?" Travis asked, following Donna into the house, tugging Autumn along with him.

"Yes. He knocked on the door and introduced himself as a friend of Autumn. He asked if I had some time to talk. I'll be honest; I've been so stir crazy lately I probably would have taken anyone up on that offer. I could tell Jamie was being genuine." She gestured to the dining room table and offered them a seat.

When they were settled Donna doled out coffee and cookies and continued talking. "I told Jamie that my son-in-law and even my husband don't seem to understand what I'm going through. I know that men grieve differently, I've heard that before, but I didn't realize it would feel so cold and distant. I thought maybe if there was anyone out there who I could connect with and who might actually understand what I was feeling, it would be you. We'd be two women destroyed by the same awful night. But Jamie was very insightful about it."

"What did he say?" Travis asked, still looking like he was being pranked.

"That no two people feel the same way in grief. If I were looking for someone who could look me in the eye and tell me they understood, I'd be looking the rest of my life. I lost my daughter that night. Sure other people have lost their children, but like Jamie said, grief is personal. There is no way to truly understand how someone else feels. But he gave me some good advice as well, maybe just trying to let me down easy."

"Advice?" Travis stammered out.

"Yes, he said I seemed like the kind of woman who really needed a cause. Which is true. I've tried to stay involved in my community and church and do things that matter. He suggested maybe there is something related to my daughter I could champion. I hadn't really thought of that. I have all this energy and no place to put it anymore. I think he was right." She sipped on her coffee and smiled.

"I'm sorry I was rejecting you while you were hurting," Autumn croaked out. "I wasn't trying to hurt you."

"I was merely projecting dear," Donna explained. "I'm angry at my son-in-law, Noah. He's completely shut me out as though we aren't family anymore now that my daughter has passed. He's a doctor and always too busy, even more so now.

I want to believe he misses my daughter, but it would help if he would show it. I'm so angry with him."

"He doesn't seem like he's hurting?" Autumn asked, completely confused by this. She had been incapable of functioning since the accident. Her life was in shambles. Wasn't his?

"It's hard to say, I guess, because I hardly see him. He works at the emergency room day and night now. He doesn't come by to see us and didn't want to hold on to any of Rayanne's things."

Autumn hadn't thrown out or given away one single thing that belonged to her husband. She couldn't bear the idea of being without something that smelled like him or that had his smudged fingerprint on it. How could this man be back at work already? How could he move on so quickly? He truly was the other half of the equation that blew their lives apart that night. So why was he better and she still a mess?

"I don't want to keep you both," Donna smiled and watched Travis check his watch again. "I heard Jamie's message loud and clear. He even offered to come by every now and then if I wanted some company. Is he your boy?" she asked, just now realizing she hadn't gotten the connection.

"Yes," Travis nodded, looking rather proud of the announcement. Likely for the first time.

"He knows a thing or two about this world for sure. You're lucky to have him as a friend, Autumn. He's really looking out for you." Donna stood and scooped up their coffee mugs.

"We'll show ourselves out," Travis assured her as he led Autumn toward the door. "I can't even wrap my head around this right now, but I'm not going to assume his plan with Paul will be the same. We need to get over there quickly."

"She seems nice," Autumn said, so quietly she wasn't even sure if Travis could hear her as they hustled to the car.

"Lots of people are nice, Autumn. You don't owe her anything. Guilt is the last thing you need right now." Travis pulled open her car door but not to be mistaken for chivalry. He was in a rush and hurrying her along.

As Travis shoved the car into gear and sped away, Autumn couldn't help but look over her shoulder at the quaint little house. The inside walls had been covered with school pictures and fond memories of a woman who died in the blink of an eye. The smashing of the two vehicles had taken this woman's life, just like it had taken Charlie's. Maybe Donna was right. Maybe they were bonded in this terrible way. How lonely it must be for her to be shut out by people in her life. What was wrong with this guy, this Noah, her son-in-law, that he couldn't even offer her any comfort? As she tried to imagine the man who had survived, just like she had, her phone began to chime.

"Is it Jamie?" Travis asked frantically.

"No," she whispered back. "It's another text message."

<u>Chapter Twenty-Two</u>

"What does it say?" Travis asked, glancing over for a second then fixing his eyes back on the road.

"*I have nothing. There's no point to this.*" Autumn read aloud as she felt a shiver go up her spine. "That makes no sense to be coming from this Paul guy. He was a dick but painfully blunt, not poetic," she reasoned.

"There," Travis announced as he pointed to Jamie's car. They both hopped out as he slammed the car into park. Travis, looking like a frantic animal, started shouting his name at the three-story walk-up apartment. "Jamie," he called loudly. "Jamie, where the hell are you?"

The screen door of the building slammed open and out fell Paul, tumbling to his hands and knees on the porch. Behind him stood Jamie with a baseball bat in hand.

"Jamie stop," Autumn begged, hitting a full sprint on her way toward the porch. "It's not him; I don't think he's sending the text messages."

"How do you know?" Jamie asked, slinging the bat to his shoulder and grinding his teeth at Paul, who was not making a move to get up.

"They don't make any sense. They're incoherent really. I don't think he's sending them." Autumn moved past Paul on the ground and stood in front of Jamie. Reaching up a hand, she placed it on the bat and stared him square in the eye. "This wasn't the kind of help I was looking for," she explained. "And I don't think he's the person sending me text messages. But I appreciate the lengths you're willing to go to for our friendship. They just aren't necessary."

He reluctantly released the bat into her hands and let his shoulders slump in disappointment. "I really wanted to bash his head in for bothering you."

"Go to hell," Paul spat back, attempting to get to his feet.

"Stay on the ground," Autumn ordered and slammed the bat inches from his knee. He plopped down and covered his head as she and Jamie walked off the porch. "You're still a complete piece of crap. Just be glad we got here in time."

Jamie fished his keys from his pocket and moved to the driver's side of his car.

"Where are you going?" Autumn asked.

"I'm not sure I want to deal with a lecture from Travis right now," he answered, gesturing to him. Travis had made his way to the foot of the porch, standing between Paul and Autumn. When Paul slinked his way back into his house Travis turned his attention back to them.

"No lecture from me," he said simply. "We need to find out who's sending these text messages. I don't know anyone better with technology than you. Three heads are better than one."

"Seriously?" Jamie asked in disbelief. "I'm about to pummel a guy with a bat, and you don't have anything to say about that? I could have ended up in prison."

"Should we go back to your house, Autumn?" Travis asked, ignoring the bait from Jamie. "Maybe if we look at all the text messages, we can come up with something."

"I've had enough excitement for one day," Autumn sighed. She ran two fingers over her throbbing temple. She needed more sleep.

"I'll drop you off then, and you can call us tomorrow." Travis placed his hand on the small of her back and led her toward the car. "Jamie," he called over his shoulder, "want to grab a bite to eat?"

"Is this a trick?" Jamie asked, still not looking convinced he was truly off the hook.

"Last chance," Travis said, one foot already inside his car.

"Fine," Jamie shrugged, "let's go grab a pizza or whatever."

Travis sank into the front seat as though he were lowering himself into a hot tub. The relief washed over him.

"I'm sorry again," she offered as Travis rested his head on the steering wheel. "I didn't mean to cause all this."

"The good news is, *all this*, turned out to be not so bad." He smiled at her. "He comforted that woman. He sat across from her and suggested she channel her grief into some actionable change. He acted like a normal human being, maybe even better than the average human being."

"He did," Autumn agreed.

"He's been listening. All this time, everything I've been saying, he's heard me. There's hope, Autumn. There's hope."

<u>Chapter Twenty-Three</u>

Noah awoke to the sound of the smoke alarm. He rolled to the side of his bed and slammed his hand down on the snooze button of his alarm clock, but the noise continued. He opened one eye, all he could muster through the fog of a hangover.

"Smoke?" he asked himself as he rolled off the bed and onto his wobbling legs. "What the hell?" He hustled through his kitchen and toward the stove. An enormous pot, the one Rayanne used to make pasta sauce on Sundays, was billowing black smoke from the top. He ran toward it, and without thinking, grabbed the pot with his bare hand and tried to lift it toward the sink. Burning himself, he jumped back and demanded his brain start functioning again.

He turned off the burner below the pot and tossed a lid over the top. Yanking open windows with his uninjured hand, he began wafting the smoke out with a kitchen towel. Grabbing the stepladder from the pantry, he positioned it under the smoke detector and ripped it from the ceiling with a primal growl. He launched it across the kitchen and the incessant noise finally ceased.

Who was cooking here, he wondered, as he looked around the kitchen at the mess that had been left behind. There were jars of empty tomato sauce and the meat that had been frozen looked like it had been sawed in half with a butcher knife. This was not the work of a skilled chef but closer to the destruction that might be left if a bear had broken in. When the pot had stopped puffing smoke from under the lid he grabbed an oven mitt and began his inspection. Lifting the lid and waving off the last bit of smoke he looked inside. At the bottom of the large pot were the remnants of chunks of steaks, the burned char of what must have been tomato sauce. *Who had done this? How had he slept through all this noise?*

Chapter Twenty-Four

Autumn slept deeply. She wasn't sure exactly how many hours she had been out, but it was still light when she'd fallen asleep, and now the sun was coming up again. Flipping off the covers she made her way for the dresser, plucked out some clean clothes, and headed to the bathroom. Spinning the knobs to the shower, she arched her back and stretched away the rest of her sleep. It wasn't until she was squirting a dollop of shampoo into her hand that she realized what had happened. She'd started her morning without hesitation. Her feet had moved, her brain had worked, and she hadn't needed to beg or bargain with herself to do it. It just happened.

The rest of the morning wasn't perfect, but she felt as though she could make it through the day, something that wasn't always a definite in her mind. At some point Travis or Jamie would call, and they'd want to come by. That didn't seem terrible. She wasn't expecting her doorbell to ring or Donna to leave yet another note for her. That was a relief. The only looming worry was the odd text messages that still didn't make any sense. She grabbed her phone and read through them again.

> *I'm so sorry for the pain I caused*
> *You shouldn't be alone. It shouldn't be this way.*
> *This is too much.*
> *I don't know where I am anymore. This has to end.*
> *How do you go on? This doesn't work.*
> *I'm so sorry. Forgive me. I don't see an answer*

Who had caused her pain? Who would believe she shouldn't be alone? Who did she need to forgive? The only person who had broken her heart was Charlie. He'd left her alone. She knew he was the kind of man who would feel sorry about that.

The house phone rang, and it sent her nearly toppling off her stool. She hurried toward it before the machine could pick up.

"Hello," she asked breathlessly.

"Hi Autumn, it's Mike. I thought I'd check in and see how you're doing."

Mike had been leaving messages for her on and off for weeks. He'd update her on his treatment and how he was feeling, and even through a recording she could tell he was lying. He and Charlie always wanted to make other people feel better, even when they were hurting.

"It's good to hear your voice, Mike," Autumn admitted, staring down at her cell phone and reading the text messages again.

"You sound well," he noticed with some excitement in his voice. "Are you feeling okay these days?"

"Good days and bad," she replied. "It's been a little hectic here honestly, but hopefully it'll settle down soon. Can I ask you something?"

"Anything," Mike said, and she could hear his smile through the phone.

"Do you think Charlie would feel bad for dying? Do you think he'd be sorry he left me alone? What if he's lost somewhere, just stuck, while he worries about how I'm doing? Doesn't that sound like him?"

"I, um, I'm not sure I follow. What do you mean stuck somewhere?" Mike's smile must have evaporated because now all she could hear was concern.

"I'm just wondering if you think Charlie would be sorry for what happened," Autumn said. She ran her finger over the screen of her cell phone to touch the words in the mysterious text messages.

"I think he would be sorry he left you," Mike answered tentatively. "But I know if one of you had to die in that accident he'd have wanted it to be him. Charlie would have wanted you to live. He'd want to see you happy again."

"Do you think he wouldn't rest until I was happy?" Autumn asked, worried she might be harming her husband in some way by drowning in her sorrow.

"Everyone has different beliefs about what happens after we die. I think Charlie is right where he is supposed to be right now. I don't think he's waiting for you to be happy before he moves on. I don't personally believe it happens that way. What has you asking all this?"

She looked down at the text messages again and considered offering him the real explanation. But instead she tossed her phone down on to the kitchen counter and leaned against the wall. "You know how it is, just too much time on my hands, sitting around and thinking."

"Have you been going to grief group," he asked, not sounding hopeful.

"Not exactly," she admitted. "I had been going for a while, but now I'm spending time with a couple people I met through the group instead. It's more comfortable for me."

"Friends?" he asked, as though it had exceeded his wildest dreams for her. It made her happy to know that when they got off the phone today he'd have some positive news to report about her.

"I guess so." She didn't want to take that away from him by explaining the odd circumstances that had formed this friendship. "How's your treatment going?" she asked, changing the subject quickly before she could ruin this for Mike.

"Slow and steady," he sighed, but she could tell his lack of elaborating likely meant things were not going so well. "I'll be out here a little longer than originally expected, but now that I know you're hanging in there it'll be easier for me to stay."

"You just get healthy," Autumn ordered. "When you get back we can celebrate."

They chatted for a few more minutes about the weather and then said their goodbyes. Autumn read the mysterious text messages again and considered the impossible. *What if this was Charlie trying to contact her?*

<u>Chapter Twenty-Five</u>

Autumn tried to look casual as she moved through the hallways of the hospital, but her nerves were showing clearly in her face. She hadn't been back here since she'd been released after the accident, and the rush of smells and sounds overloaded her senses. Why she even wanted to find this man was hard to pinpoint.

Her conversation with Donna about her son-in-law, Noah, had been lingering in her mind all day. They had more in common than she was willing to admit before, but now it was impossible not to face it. He survived the crash. So did she. He lost his spouse. So did she. Their lives were changed forever at the exact same second. That had to mean something.

How had he found a way to move on so quickly? He was working, living his life, while she had to coax herself into brushing her teeth. She still couldn't get behind the driver's wheel of a car. But he was somehow saving lives in the emergency room again? She had to see it for herself. Maybe he knew something she didn't.

"Excuse me," Autumn asked timidly. The nurse behind the desk was reading her computer screen intently and didn't stop as she answered.

"May I help you?"

"I'm looking for Dr. Noah Key," she explained and took note of how quickly the nurse gave her her undivided attention.

"Are you a patient of his? Because Dr. Lopez is covering all his patients now." She cocked an eyebrow up and looked as though she were waiting for something interesting to happen.

"I'm not a patient. He and I have a mutual friend, and I was hoping to see him today. What's the next day he'll be working?" Autumn fiddled with the strap of her purse as she waited for the answer. The look on the nurse's face didn't make much sense for this seemingly innocuous request.

The nurse leaned in closer, and the corners of her mouth rose up slightly, not quite a smile but close. Her eyes danced like those of a child about to spill a secret. "No one is sure when or if he'll be back. He kind of lost it." Her voice was low but the heads of the nurses next to her perked up slightly.

"What do you mean he lost it?" Autumn asked, annoyed by this gossipy excitement but still wanting answers. The way Donna had explained, Noah hadn't had any problems since losing his wife.

"Well there were multiple incidents, but I really shouldn't say much more about it," the nurse leaned in another inch, begging for Autumn to push for more information.

"So he's not working here anymore?" Autumn asked.

"They're saying indefinite suspension but since there are drugs involved I don't see a way they'd ever bring him back. No one liked him that much to begin with." A few of the other nurses nodded their head in agreement, and it was infuriating Autumn.

"He lost his wife," she reminded them, a little bite in her tone.

"Oh we know," the nurse said, covering her heart with one hand. "That was so sad; it really pushed him over the edge. A shame really."

None of their faces looked even remotely sad. She felt a bubble of anger rise from her toes and settle in her core. "You are insensitive, gossiping, heartless bitches, and I hope you never have something terrible happen to you, making the people around you respond so harshly." She turned abruptly and stormed toward the door before any of the women could pick their jaws off the floor and reply.

She whispered angrily to herself as she hustled to the car. What the hell was going on with this Noah guy? Drugs? Suspended? This wasn't at all what Donna had described.

The screen of her phone chirped to life, and she dug it out of her purse. There was a brief moment of hope that maybe it was another mystery text message. The logical part of her brain was still fighting to tell her heart it was completely impossible for Charlie to be trying to contact her. But just like the first time she'd met Charlie, there were butterflies in her stomach every time the thought of him reaching out crossed her mind. The same way love wasn't always logical, navigating loss didn't follow the straightest path either.

But the text wasn't mysterious at all. It was Travis. *Jamie and I have been talking about those text messages, and we have a few ideas. Come get a bite to eat?*

A knot of nerves tightened in her stomach as she thought about trying to explain what she was thinking about the messages to Travis. He was such a logical man. He'd probably want to call the funny farm on her again if she started talking about text messages from beyond the grave.

She stared at her phone and tried to think of a tactful way to decline, but nothing came to her. *Sounds good*, she replied.

Chapter Twenty-Six

"What do you mean forget about the text messages?" Jamie asked with a mouthful of cheeseburger. "You were just freaking out about this yesterday."

"I haven't gotten any in a while, and I'm just going to change my number. Let's forget about it," Autumn stared down at her salad and moved the lettuce around absentmindedly.

"Are you sure?" Travis jumped in before Jamie could make an insensitive argument. "We'll take your lead on this."

"But," Jamie contended, "don't you want to know what kind of creep is sending you the messages? You should at least let us read them."

"I already deleted them," Autumn lied.

"Really?" Travis asked. "So you do want to let this go? Jamie is savvy with computers; he might be able to find the source easily."

"Yeah, if they have their number blocked there are still plenty of things to do," Jamie explained. "Even now that you deleted them I can still get some info."

"I, well . . . no really, I think I should let this go. Let's talk about something else. I went to the hospital today."

"Why, what's the matter?" Travis asked, looking her over like she was hiding some physical injury he'd overlooked.

"Nothing," she chuckled. "I went to see Noah Key. I wanted to see how he was doing."

"Why?" Travis asked, tilting his head in confusion. "You were so determined to keep these people at bay, and you went there to see him?"

"I told you, Travis," Jamie grunted as he dipped his fries in his pile of ketchup. "Chicks are nuts. They say one thing and do another. You can't try to figure them out; it'll make your head spin."

130

Travis opened his mouth to scold Jamie about his ignorant opinion, but Autumn cut in with a joke that broke the tension.

"Bitches be crazy," she said in a deep voice and picked up her beer, took a long swig, then banged her glass against Jamie's as though they were in complete agreement.

"Exactly!" Jamie agreed, raising his glass before taking a long sip of his soda. Every time they'd eaten together he'd tried to order a beer, but Travis would cut in and change it to a soda. Autumn had originally seen this as a conflict between them but was starting to realize it was something very innocent that had somehow morphed into a habit.

"So anyway," Travis interrupted, shaking his head at their ridiculousness, "what did Noah say?"

"He wasn't there. The nurses gave me an earful about how he's suspended indefinitely from the hospital. Something about multiple incidences and maybe even some drugs. Very bizarre, considering that's not the impression I got from Donna about him."

"People are fake," Jamie announced. "You can pretend to be anyone you want, and most people will fall for it."

Travis smiled, and Autumn knew he was thinking about Jamie sitting across from Donna, eating cookies and chatting. "You're full of wisdom today," he teased.

"All I'm saying is this guy can walk around making people think he's all fine or whatever, but you can't be completely off the rails and think no one will notice. If the dude's on drugs, of course he gonna get caught. That's why I don't bother trying to be anything I'm not. I drink, I get messed up, and I say shit no one wants to hear. But I'm not trying to fool anyone."

"And you're doing a wonderful job of not trying to be anything better," Autumn joked. "Don't set the bar too high or anything."

"I'm not hurting anyone," Jamie said with a shrug as he finished off the rest of his cheeseburger.

"Right," Autumn coughed out. "You're just giving Travis high-blood pressure and putting countless lives in danger by driving drunk."

"Whoa," Jamie said, raising his hands disarmingly. "So far I've threatened a guy with a bat for you and dragged you out of a very dark place. Don't go hating on me now. All I'm saying is at least I own my stuff. This guy sounds like a complete ass, trying to just go to work like nothing's going on and being cold to his mother-in-law. Now he's doing drugs and still trying to be a doctor. That's a scumbag."

"You really did have a long conversation with Donna didn't you?" Autumn asked, cocking an eyebrow at him. So far no one had brought up they knew Jamie had been to her house. No one had mentioned how sweet she found him and how helpful he'd been. She could see by the expression on Jamie's face he hoped that fact was still buried.

"Whatever," he grumbled. It was so odd to Autumn he was more comfortable talking about what a mess he was, than about how nice he'd been to someone.

"So what are you going to do with this Noah situation, just let it go too?" Travis asked, protectively deflecting the attention away from Jamie.

"I'm not even sure why I care," Autumn admitted. "I just keep wondering what it's been like for him. Our situations are so similar. He was there that night. Maybe he remembers more than I do. Maybe he can tell me what happened."

"Your husband got killed, that's what happened. What else do you need to know?" Jamie gestured to the waiter to bring another soda.

"Jamie, for hell's sake," Travis grunted, slamming his beer down. "You need like a lobotomy or something. You can't say everything that comes to your mind."

"No, he's kind of right," Autumn said, raising a hand to calm Travis. "It's not going to change anything. I just need to put it behind me. I don't know why I can't think straight anymore." She rested her head in her hand and sighed.

"It's normal," Travis assured her. "Go with your gut, but be cautious. He might not really be interested in talking. And if he's using drugs . . ." Travis trailed off.

"I hear you," Autumn said, agreeing that reaching out to Noah might be a bad idea for a lot of reasons.

Her phone vibrated in her pocket and her heart skipped a beat. "I'll be right back, just going to run to the bathroom."

She slid her chair back quickly and it nearly toppled over behind her. "You good?" Jamie asked, catching the chair before it hit the floor.

"Yep," she smiled, racing away from the table. Before she even hit the bathroom door, she was pulling out her phone. The text message read, *If I could change it all I would. I'm sorry it's too late.*

"Charlie?" she whispered to herself, holding the phone to her heart as she tried to keep it together.

When the screen went dark she tapped it, bringing the message back to a glowing lifeline. She wondered if she should reply. Did it work that way? Was that possible?

It's not your fault she keyed in and hit send before she could talk herself out of it. Waiting for another minute she prayed for a response. She wanted a volley of dialog to pass between them, even if she wasn't certain what she should say. But a couple minutes passed and nothing. She knew Travis and Jamie would be wondering where she was now. Tucking her phone away, she drew in a deep breath and headed to the table.

"Did you fall in?" Jamie teased, sliding a spoon toward her and gesturing down at the ice cream sundae the three of them were going to split.

"I'm surprised you saved me some; you're a bottomless pit." She settled into her chair and dug into dessert. Life was messy. Things were confusing, and every day something hurt, either physically or deep in her heart. But she had to admit, chocolate and whipped cream could, for a split second, heal it all.

Chapter Twenty-Seven

Noah could smell vomit, but he wasn't sure why. Working at the ER meant all bodily fluids were cataloged by scent in his brain. As his eyes cracked open, he realized why the smell was so strong; he was lying in a puddle of it.

"Damn it," he groaned and rolled off the floor of his bedroom and onto his feet. His head was not just throbbing, it was banging, like his brain was trying to escape. Everything was foggy.

When you had no job it was very easy to lose track of simple things like what day it was. If he looked it up and realized it was Tuesday, he'd be just as surprised as if it were Sunday. He couldn't remember the last time he ate, though he was sure if he spent enough time evaluating the vomit on the floor he could figure it out. At least the smoke alarm wasn't blaring today.

Before the accident he'd wake up every morning at five thirty and hop on the treadmill. Then he'd spend half an hour on his phone, reading the news, and checking email. Now it was easy to go hours without even glancing at his phone. No one from work would be calling with a question about a patient. Donna had given up trying to reach out to him. And the news wasn't that interesting anymore when his life was falling apart.

He peeled away his clothes and tossed them directly into the overflowing trashcan. What the hell had become of him, he wondered as he stepped into the shower. Something had to give. He couldn't just sit around, drowning in booze and pills.

After a long hot shower and some clean clothes, he felt like maybe he could face the day. Grabbing a fresh trash bag, he moved around his house, rounding up the takeout containers and empty bottles of Scotch. With a bucket of hot soapy water, he scrubbed the floor. He had never really cleaned this house before. Rayanne always had. She kept everything in order.

When he reached for something, it was always there, always stocked or clean. She made their home run efficiently so he could go into work every day and be the best doctor he could be. Rayanne made his life work, and living without her was like running an engine without oil. Everything was grinding to a halt, and irreparable damage was being done with each second that ticked by.

Grabbing a broom from the pantry, he started sweeping the kitchen floor. There was just one thing in the way: a large box filled with all his wife's personal thoughts and feelings from the last fifteen years. If the box weighed twenty pounds physically, it weighed a ton emotionally.

He used the broom to flip open one flap of the box, and he looked down at the bright flowered covers of the journals. Reaching in, he grabbed one, half expecting to get electrocuted or burned by touching it. But nothing happened. When he opened the book it didn't burst into flames. He was face to face with his wife's familiar and beautiful scrawl. It was dated eleven years ago, before the two of them had met. Doing the math, he realized she'd have been studying abroad in Paris. She'd told him endless stories about her time there and always hinted at wanting to go back with him someday. She wanted to show him all the cafés she'd sat in while she was designing outfits. He'd heard so many of the stories, but he couldn't recall them, and he knew it was because he wasn't really listening.

She'd spoken so many words to him over the years, and how many had really registered with him? What were her friends' names again? That coffee shop she liked, what was that pastry thing she used to get when she was feeling homesick? Why couldn't he remember the tiny details that all came together to form the woman he loved? There was no doubt in his mind he loved Rayanne more than anyone else in his life. But maybe loving someone as well as he could was not the same as loving them enough. Maybe his best was still a pale comparison to the way other husbands treated their wives.

He gave up fighting the urge to avert his eyes from the page. He wanted to know what he'd missed by being busy all these years.

Paris is the source of all my joy. I will leave a piece of myself in this city and come back to claim it someday when I have grown into the person I'm meant to be. I will never again have the chance to look at this magical place with that first time excitement, but maybe someday I'll have someone to share it with. That will be its own kind of magic. Being here has been like a rebirthing of sorts, but I know the only thing that would make this any better would be having a hand to hold as I walk down these streets. Or to have someone to kiss at midnight on New Year's Eve under the Eiffel Tower. I know anyone I love will have to love this place as well.

He slammed the book closed and threw it back into the box. Rayanne never went back to Paris. A year after she got back to the States she had the unfortunate luck to meet Noah. Within a year they were married, and Rayanne was transformed from a free-spirited ball of energy to a doctor's wife, determined to help Noah advance his career. He'd become front and center in her life. She gave up everything she loved to love him. Not all at once because surely that would have raised some alarm in her mind. She was like a bucket with a tiny crack, her hopes and dreams seeping out a little at a time until she was empty.

In his defense it wasn't calculated. He hadn't asked her to stop designing clothes, not specifically. He'd just told her the truth when she asked. His answer to her question about whether she should stick with it was simply no. There was no need to. Their income was solid, so why clutter up the spare room with fabrics and mannequins? And a few months later the room had been cleared out. When they did vacation—which was rare, considering the only real rush Noah got came from the emergency room—they always went where he wanted to go. Shouldn't it be his choice of destination since he was putting in the long hours and the hard work? Hadn't

Rayanne said that, or was it he who'd made that point? So they'd ended up on a sandy beach on some quiet island where he could gamble late into the night, just trying to feel his blood pressure rise with a thrill. He'd lose. They'd argue. Vacation over. It was the same every time.

She'd hinted at Paris. Or at least he was pretty sure she had. But like everything else, eventually she just stopped bringing it up. But wait, Noah thought, trying to redeem himself a little. They had the money, and he'd always been very clear that it was their money, not his. If she wanted a trip to Paris she could have gone at any time. *But whose hand would she have held as she strolled down the street?*

He'd robbed her. Her life had great potential and instead, little by little, he stole it away by making his priorities far superior to her desires. There was something far worse than the trips to Paris they never took or the career she never followed. There was something he'd stolen from her that was far worse than any of those things, and he'd have to live with the regret for the rest of his life. But maybe that wouldn't be so long.

He kicked at the box, sending it flying into the wall. It was as though he was on trial, and this was the evidence to condemn him. In her own words was the irrefutable reality he'd wrecked his wife's life, and now that she was dead there was no way to make it right. He grabbed at the bottle of pills he swore he was going to flush down the drain and rattled a few into his hand. He shook out a couple more and popped them all into his mouth. He was a wrecking ball, and it was time to cut the chain before he hurt anyone else.

Before the pills could rush relief to his body he heard his phone chirp with a message. Snatching it from the table with a shaking hand he threw it into the sink. The chirp rang out and then got swallowed up by the soapy water. He stumbled back toward his bed, grabbing a bottle of vodka on the way. Sleep. He just wanted to sleep.

<u>Chapter Twenty-Eight</u>

She'd screwed it up. The whole thing was over now, and it was because of her. Autumn paced around her front yard because there wasn't enough air in the house to keep her from hyperventilating. She'd had this line to her husband, and she lost it because she was too stupid to realize she shouldn't take the chance of texting him back. That would screw up the delicate cosmos that had aligned to make this all possible.

"Autumn?" Jamie asked, stepping next to her. Though she was sure he hadn't been quiet as he approached, she hadn't heard a thing.

"What are you doing here?" she asked, feeling too overwhelmed to chat.

"You were supposed to meet me after my AA meeting tonight. Remember, we were going to get Travis something for his birthday? I know it was lame, but if you didn't want to go you should have texted me or something. I was waiting like an hour."

"Oh, sorry," she said, still not looking at him.

"Why are you walking around on the lawn in your pajamas?" he asked, looking around as though the answer might become clear to him if he could see what she saw.

"I needed air," she replied, nervously wringing her hands together. "I just, something happened. I did something stupid, and I needed some air. I couldn't breathe." Her chest grew tighter as she thought of never hearing from Charlie again. She'd already come to terms with that once, but this little flicker of hope was dashed again, and it hurt as much as the first time she'd lost him.

Clutching at her chest, she gasped for air. She felt Jamie's arm close in around her and guide her toward the house.

"What did you do that was so stupid? We can fix it, whatever it was," Jamie assured her. She stared at him curiously. How could someone so selfish and destructive know so well how to speak to a frantic woman?

"He was sending me text messages," she stuttered out. "Charlie was sending messages to my phone, and I was stupid, and I texted back. Of course that wouldn't work. It doesn't work that way, right?" She looked at Jamie as though he might know the secret rules of the paranormal world. His face should have been twisted up in confusion or his eyes wide with worry, but they weren't. He just nodded his head and led her through the door and toward the couch.

"You think the messages you were getting were from your husband?" Jamie asked, sitting on the coffee table and leaning close to her.

"Yes," she replied adamantly. "I know it was him. It has to be. And I got greedy, I wanted to hear from him, and ask him so many questions. But now I've ruined it."

Jamie took her hands in his and clutched them tightly, trying to get all of her attention on him and only him. "I'm sure you didn't ruin it. I'm sure we can still fix it. Can I see your phone?"

This was not how Autumn assumed this would go. A cynical unfiltered guy like Jamie would hear this idea about the text messages and scoff or downright insult her. Instead he was trying to calm her and sort this out.

She reached into her pajama pants pocket and handed over her phone. "I know I told you I deleted them. Once I knew they were from Charlie I didn't want to tell you. I thought you'd say I was crazy."

"I hate that word," Jamie said, staring her straight in the eye as he reluctantly let go of her hands.

He flipped through the messages and read them carefully. She watched his face stay flat and unemotional, not reacting one way or the other.

"I can do a quick diagnostic test on your phone and try to find out more about the text messages if you want me to. I think we should know more." Jamie was flipping through her phone quickly.

"What could you possibly find out?" Autumn asked as though it were Jamie who was being crazy to think any type of earthly technology would be able to reconnect what she had broken.

"I don't know," Jamie shrugged. "If they aren't from Charlie, they might be from someone who needs help. And if they are from Charlie, then maybe I can find a way to get him to send another message."

"They're from Charlie. Look at them." She pointed frantically at the screen and insisted he scroll up to the top.

"Okay," Jamie said, nodding his head, but she was starting to think he was just appeasing her. Did he actually think they could be from her dead husband? Did he believe it? "So I'm going to call Travis and have him come by. He'll know what to do."

"No," she shouted, snatching the phone back. "You know he won't believe this. He's not that kind of person. He'll think I'm losing it. I can't deal with him right now."

"Listen," Jamie said, standing up and taking a few steps back to give her space she didn't even realize she needed. "I won't call Travis, but then you have to hear me out. I'm not saying these aren't from Charlie, but will you at least agree there is a chance they are not?"

She bit at her lip as she thought it over. "There's a chance they aren't, I guess," she admitted. "I want them to be though, Jamie. I want them to be."

"I know," he said softly. "But if they aren't, they could be interpreted in kind of a dark way, you know what I mean?"

"No," Autumn said, looking at the messages again.

"This person, if it's not Charlie, sounds like they don't want to live anymore. They sound like they have a lot of guilt about something, and they might want to you know," Jamie said, but Autumn didn't light with understanding. "They might want to kill themselves. It sounds like that."

"What?" Autumn scoffed. "No they don't. This is Charlie feeling bad for leaving me. This is him wishing things were different."

"Maybe," Jamie said, trying to look convincing in his partial agreement. "But I've kind of been in a spot like this before," Jamie stuttered out uncomfortably. "It sounds familiar. I can kind of read between the lines, and whoever it is might need help."

"No," Autumn said adamantly. "No it's Charlie."

Jamie moved toward her and sat again on the coffee table. He reached for her hands, but she recoiled, not wanting him to take the phone. He tried again, but this time more gently, so she couldn't help but allow him to rest his hand on hers. "You're right," he agreed. "I think it's probably Charlie too. But what if Charlie is trying to get you to help someone? What if he knows you are the kind of person who wouldn't want someone to hurt themselves? You don't, right?"

"Of course not." She shook her head, sending the tears that had been balancing on her lashes trailing down her face.

"Then maybe Charlie wants you to help. Maybe he wants you to do something, and that's why he sent these messages. If you let me have your phone we can find out what Charlie wanted you to do."

"He wouldn't want anyone to hurt themselves. Charlie always helped people when he could. I guess maybe if you really think that's what's going on, you should check it out." She reluctantly handed the phone over, hesitating on her decision as his hand took hold of it.

"I promise I'll give it right back, and all the messages will still be there. I have to grab my laptop and some stuff out of my car. Just wait here."

A few minutes later Jamie was set up at the kitchen table and plugging the phone into his computer.

"Why do you have all that stuff?" Autumn asked, checking out the unfamiliar contraptions he had lined up next to his laptop.

"I've done some stupid things over the years with not so great people. It helps to be able to get the edge over them sometimes. Lots of these tough guys are all muscle and no brain. I developed a few skills to help me get leverage when I needed it."

"I don't even know what you mean," Autumn said. She grabbed a glass and filled it with water for him.

"For example, if maybe I was distributing some merchandise for someone and they were putting pressure on me to perform faster for them and their expectations weren't reasonable, I'd hack into their system, download all their files or bank statements that showed where they were funneling their money, and let them know to back off."

"What?" Autumn asked, shaking her head in confusion.

"If I was selling drugs for someone, and they got crazy on me, I'd threaten to leak all their important info. It's not very classy, but it's insurance."

"You sell drugs?" Autumn asked, looking him up and down as though he should have more telltale signs of this job.

"Not right now I don't. It was when I was a kid. I do other things to make money now," he explained and began typing hurriedly, clicking buttons on the phone.

"You needed the money as a kid?" she asked, knowing where her question was leading.

"These calls are coming from a cell phone that's using an app that blocks the number. It's not fancy, pretty easy to back into the information. I just need a few more minutes."

"But," Autumn furrowed her brow, "I thought that . . ." she trailed off as she watched Jamie focus solely on the task at hand. "No," she said firmly. "Then stop. I don't want you to do this anymore. Just give me back my phone." She lunged for him, but he blocked her with his forearm.

"Autumn, please give me a minute. I know you're confused and upset, but I need to do this. Just sit down."

"No!" she cried, slamming her hand against his shoulder, trying to shove him out of the way so she could get her phone unplugged. She accidently knocked over the glass of water. He grabbed his computer and the phone hooked to it and backed away from her. He moved toward the bathroom and closed the door.

"Stop," she pleaded. "Please don't do this Jamie. Please don't tell me these aren't from Charlie. I need them to be."

"I'm sorry, Autumn," he apologized through the locked door she was banging on.

A few minutes later, when her hand was stinging from banging on the door, she gave up. She slithered her body over toward the couch and buried her face in a pillow. When she heard the squeaky hinges of the bathroom door creak open she rolled her head to the side so she could see him.

"I'm really sorry, Autumn," he whispered.

"Who are they from," she croaked, looking utterly defeated.

"Noah Key," Jamie explained as he stared down at his shoes. "That's the guy right? The doctor who survived the accident that night?"

She wiped at her nose and eyes with the sleeve of her shirt and let the information infiltrate her brain slowly. Noah Key had been sending her anonymous text messages apologizing to her? Why? He hadn't caused the accident. It was the weather and the winding road. "You think he sounds like he's going to hurt himself?" Autumn asked as she pulled herself slowly back up to a sitting position.

"Yes," Jamie said flatly.

"How do you know?" she asked, narrowing her aching eyes at him.

"My mother . . . she—" he stopped abruptly and cleared his throat. "I just know what it sounds like. He's talking about it being too much for him. He's talking about ending it. Not going on. I'm not saying it's imminent or anything, I'm just saying he might need help."

"So what are we supposed to do?" Autumn asked, throwing her hands up. A spear had just been launched at her heart; was she supposed to just pull it out, get up and go help someone else? She couldn't even help herself. She wasn't entirely certain she wasn't on the same exact path as this man, Noah.

"Let me call Travis. Please," Jamie pleaded. "I don't know what to do, but he will."

"Don't you ever do anything for yourself Jamie? You depend on him for everything. That man will never be happy as long as you keep bringing him messes to have to clean up over and over again. You are pulling him through the mud, and you don't even care about him." She'd never actually spat in someone's face before. It was a vile gesture but right now she was considering it.

"Autumn," Jamie sighed, finally raising his eyes up to hers. "I know I'm a piece of shit. I know exactly what I've done to Travis, and for the life of me, I don't know why he keeps trying to save me. I don't want to be saved. I don't want to stop hating myself. But this is different."

"How?" Autumn argued.

"Because I don't call Travis when I'm in trouble, he just shows up. I don't ask him to help me out, he just insists. If I call him right now, for the first time I'd actually be doing the right thing. This is what he'd want me to do, and I'm actually going to."

"Leave me out of it," Autumn demanded, as she stormed by him and headed toward the stairs. She wasn't anyone's life preserver right now. She was an anchor. The only thing she could do was sink them to the bottom a little faster.

Chapter Twenty-Nine

It took Noah four times to correctly load his gun and seven tries to get the key in the ignition of his car. Double vision wouldn't have been so bad, but he was pretty sure he was seeing four of everything at this point. The note he'd scribbled out probably wasn't even coherent but he owed Donna something. It would have been just one more selfish act to kill himself now and not give her a tiny crumb of truth. He'd never understand the woman, but she was a far better person than he was. The fact that she even tolerated him in her daughter's life was a testament to her capacity for kindness.

He pushed every thought out of his head and focused on navigating his car. It took every ounce of his attention to keep it between the lines. The radio played a song, but he couldn't hear it. The wind blew on his face, but he couldn't feel it. The air was filled with the scent of blooming flowers, but he couldn't smell them. Maybe he was already dead. Wouldn't that be easy?

<u>Chapter Thirty</u>

Autumn's phone rang incessantly for five minutes until finally she gave in and answered it. "I said leave me out of this, Jamie," she shouted angrily.

"Autumn, it's Travis," he spat out frantically, ignoring her crossness. "Jamie and I just went by Noah's house and the door was open. He wasn't there but he'd left a note. I think he's going to hurt himself. There was a box of bullets left open on the table. I'm going to send a buddy of mine who's a police officer over to your house just in case. I'm sure Noah isn't looking to harm anyone else, but since he was reaching out to you by text message I want to be sure. Jamie and I will be there as soon as we can."

"Where is Noah?" Autumn asked, feeling like the cops should be heading to the guy with the gun who left a suicide note instead of to her.

"They've put a BOLO out for him and his vehicle. I'm sure they'll find him. Like I said, nothing in the note alluded to him wanting to hurt anyone else but just to be safe."

"What did the note say?" Autumn asked, walking over to her window and peering through the sheer curtains.

"I'm, I can't really remember," he stuttered out. Travis was a terrible liar.

"I want to know Travis, what did the note say?" Autumn insisted.

"He was apologizing to Donna for the pain he caused to her daughter. Not in the accident but all the time leading up to that night. He was sorry for all the things she'd given up to be with him. He was going to make it right. He was going to change it and make it happen the way it should have. It was kind of gibberish towards the end really."

"Tell Jamie . . ." Autumn started but wasn't sure how to finish. She wasn't sorry. She wasn't forgiving him. Everything still hurt, like her body had been scratched raw. But something needed to be said.

"I'll tell him," Travis assured her. "Just sit tight."

When she hung up the phone she stepped outside and looked up toward the sky. "Charlie, I wanted those messages to be from you. I wanted you to be telling me something. I needed to hear from you. I'm so alone." A bird chirped back a reply and the leaves in a nearby tree rustled, but she couldn't hear Charlie's voice. That was the only thing that would make her feel better. "How can he think he's going to make this right?" she asked, still speaking her words up to the sky. "He can't change anything. He can't make it happen the way he thinks it was supposed to. He can't bring her back to life."

Like a whisper in her ear it struck her. Noah should have died that night. That's what he would change. Out there on the dark road he should have taken his last breath not his wife. That's where he would go to do it. She should call Travis or tell the officer coming to her house to drive the twenty minutes to that quiet stretch of road and stop Noah from killing himself. But what would they say? Could they really understand what Noah was feeling? They weren't there that night. They wouldn't understand. But she would.

She raced back into her house, kicked off her slippers and squeezed her feet into her sneakers. Grabbing her car keys she hurried toward her driveway and stopped suddenly. She hadn't driven in months. She couldn't. And she certainly shouldn't let the first time she drove be back to the place that it had all happened. This was crazy. The man had a gun. The police were equipped to handle this, not her.

But under her feet crackled the broken pieces of the pot she'd launched at Travis. She was not healed. She was not well, and she knew that if anyone's words could reach Noah, hers had the best chance.

Gritting her teeth and forcing her legs forward she got in her car, started the engine, and barreled out of her driveway. Her hands were steadier than she imagined they would be. She might be driving to face a man who'd lost his mind and was wielding a gun. But she was driving.

Her phone started ringing a few minutes after she left the house. Travis would think the worst when his buddy got there, and she and her car were gone. He'd lose his mind with worry. She waited until she was just a minute or so from the accident scene before picking up.

"I'm okay Travis," she said rather than hello.

"Where are you? You were supposed to stay home. Your car is gone. Are you driving?"

"Yes," she replied, trying to sound calm. "I think I know where Noah is going. I think he's going to the accident scene. That's where he's going to do it."

"How do you know that?" Travis asked but then changed his question abruptly. "Are you going there? Tell me you aren't going there now?"

"I'm going to be there in a minute. I'll talk to him. I understand how he feels." She squeezed the phone tightly in her hand as she heard Travis start to fall apart. She wasn't trying to scare him or hurt him, but it was unavoidable. He cared for her, and she was taking an enormous risk. Before he could cut in with his logic she hung up, unrolled her window, and tossed her phone out.

Rounding the corner, she gasped as she was transported back to the night Charlie died. She remembered the yellow guardrail and fallen tree that lay behind it. Just over the crest of the next hill was where it happened. This was the last stretch of road where her life made sense. This was the last place she and Charlie were both still alive. It took only a few seconds to crest the hill and put that stretch of road behind her.

There off to the side of the otherwise deserted road was a car. Its driver door was swung wide open and a man sat kneeling by it. Autumn pressed the accelerator down hard, closed the gap, and pulled her car behind his.

"Noah," she yelled, practically falling out of her car as she slammed it in park. "Noah don't."

"Rayanne," Noah mouthed and Autumn's heart broke. She wasn't the only one hurting bad enough to believe what death had taken could somehow be returned.

"My name is Autumn," she said, losing her breath as she caught a glimpse of black metal in his hand. "I was here that night too. Do you know who I am?"

She rounded the front of the car cautiously and tried to get a better glimpse at his face, but the sharpness in his voice had her freezing in her tracks.

"Don't come over here. I know who you are." She watched as his knuckles grew white, his grip on the gun as tight as a vice.

"I'm not going to come any closer," Autumn promised, putting her hands up and trying to get his attention, but he was too focused on what he'd come for.

"Why are you here?" he barked.

"I got the text messages you sent me. You were trying to tell me you were hurting, right? Well, I was listening."

"I, that's not what I was doing," Noah slurred out. "I was telling you I was sorry. I just sent one, thinking you'd never even know it was me. The rest I was just blacked out for. I didn't even mean to," he trailed off as he waved his free hand at her to go away.

"I know what you're feeling right now. But you don't have to be sorry. The accident was just that, an accident. It was dark and the weather was so bad."

"I ruined your life, and I wrecked hers," Noah bellowed. "She was so perfect and full of life, and I destroyed that. Rayanne never should have married me."

"The regret, I feel it too." Autumn slid her feet slowly, an inch closer and then another. "Every stupid argument I had with Charlie, every minute I wasted being upset about something."

"You don't get it," Noah said in a breathy exasperated laugh. "I shattered her. She wanted this life, this magical fairytale life, and I made her live in the real world. I spent all my time reminding her to be logical and realistic."

"I'm sure she loved you. You were out on New Year's Eve just like Charlie and me. She obviously wanted to be with you."

"Stay," he said, turning the gun toward her and spitting as he yelled. "Don't try to come down here."

"Okay," she assured him, going as still as a statue. "I don't understand; can you tell me why you think you ruined her life?"

"That night," he choked out, "she was just sipping one glass of wine. I should have picked up on it. So in the car when she started asking me about our future and having kids I told her for the hundredth time it wasn't what I wanted out of my life. She knew that before we married. But I should have known even if she were agreeing to that at the time, she'd regret it. Rayanne would have been the most incredible mother." He raised the gun back up to his temple and stared up at the sky.

"Charlie and I never had kids either. We just kept putting it off. I wake up every morning wondering if I would feel differently if I had this little piece of him here with me. A tiny little face that reminded me of him."

"She was pregnant," Noah said, coughing through tears. "That's what she was trying to tell me. That's why she was so angry when I snapped at her for bringing up the idea of kids again. We were screaming at each other. Then she just blurted it out. Thirty seconds later she was sitting next to me in a heap of twisted metal—dead." Autumn watched his thumb pull down the piece of metal, and while she didn't know the technical term for it, she'd seen enough movies to know that move came right before pulling the trigger.

"Noah, stop please," she started toward him in a hurried walk that turned into a run. "Please don't do this." She slid to her knees in front of him and ignored the gravel that ripped her pajama pants and scraped her skin. Nose to nose, she stared into his eyes and begged him again. "I don't know your wife, and I don't know you, but we were all here that night. We've all been changed."

"Who cares; why are you here?" He narrowed his eyes, and she watched sweat pour down his forehead.

"Four people were here that night, and two of us survived. No one knows what it was like that night more than you. Don't leave me alone in this. If you really think you screwed up your wife's whole life, and you are dying from the guilt, then don't do the same to me. Don't shoot yourself in the head right in front of me."

"Then go," he yelled, his booming voice hurting her ears. "If you don't want to see this then go." The smell of alcohol on his breath stung her tear-filled eyes.

"Your wife had a choice, Noah. She didn't have to stay married to you. There's no way to know how she felt, but the fact that she stayed with you means something."

"Telling someone you're pregnant should be the happiest moment of your life, and I stole that from her by being a selfish prick. And in the last seconds of your life you deserve peace. I stole that from her too. I don't deserve to live."

She watched his finger dance on the trigger. "You live, or you die, Noah. Those are your two choices. If you really want to do justice to your wife, figure out which one she would have wanted, and for once, let her have a say in it. If you took away all her other choices, give her this one. What would she want you to do?"

For the first time his glossy frantic eyes focused on her face. It was as if she'd just slapped sense back into his head, and everything, for a brief second, made sense.

"She hated guns," he croaked as he took the weapon off his temple and lowered it. "She begged me not to get one, but I did anyway."

Autumn reached across and placed her hand over the cool metal. He was still gripping it tightly when she whispered again, "Give her the choice." His hand went limp and Autumn snatched away the gun, the first she'd ever held. An impulse reaction came over her, and she cocked her arm back and launched it into the woods. She wanted it as far away from them as she could get it.

"This hurts," Noah admitted and leaned forward into Autumn's arms. "I'm in this storm, wind and rain pelting my body all day long. I just want it to stop."

"Storms always stop eventually." Autumn tried to assure him, squeezing him as tight as her arms would allow. "They pass; they get weaker. Maybe it's always going to rain on us, but some days it won't be so hard."

They heard a roaring car engine, pushed to its limits, coming over the hill. A skidding stop and a flash of red were the only two things that registered with her before she heard Travis's voice calling her name.

"We're over here," she called, but her vocal cords were trembling just as her whole body was now.

"Jesus," she heard Jamie say as they both skidded to a stop in the gravel and looked down at her and Noah, kneeling in the dirt.

"The police are on their way," Travis said calmly, and she could feel his eyes all over her, checking to see if she were hurt or if the danger were still looming.

"The gun is in the woods," she assured him as she turned her head and looked up at him finally. Noah's body was shaking with emotion, and his head was planted firmly on her shoulder. Travis reached a hand out to lift her, but she gave a slight shake of her head to wave him off. She wasn't letting him go. If he wanted to sit here all night and ache, she'd be right there to do the same. Because they'd both lost everything right in this spot at the very same moment. And if he were in the storm right now, then she'd sit in the rain with him.

<u>Chapter Thirty-One</u>

An EMT who knew Noah from the hospital finally convinced him to get off the ground. When he'd been lifted into the back of the ambulance, he finally let go of Autumn's hand.

"I can ride with you," she offered, making a move to climb into the back if that's what he wanted.

"No," he said, his eyes still closed. "You already did the hard stuff; the rest of this I can do on my own."

"You don't have to. We don't have to be alone in this, Noah." She held a hand to the open ambulance door so she couldn't be shut out before the conversation was done.

"You're not alone," Noah said, finally slitting his eyes open a fraction of the way and gesturing to Travis and Jamie, who were standing a few feet behind her. She looked over her shoulder and saw the concern on their faces. "You'll make it through the storm," he said, nodding his head. "You have a couple of umbrellas."

Before she could reply and assure him that he could too, the EMT moved her backward and closed the door. The lights on the top of the ambulance came alive, and it pulled back onto the road, quickly disappearing over the hill.

"What the hell happened?" Jamie asked, running his hand over his head, trying to compute all of this insanity.

"I just didn't want him to hurt himself." Autumn's adrenaline-powered strength was draining. She wobbled a bit on her feet, and Travis caught her elbow.

"He could have hurt you and then himself. There were drugs involved and a gun. This was not a good idea." Travis was looking sternly at her.

"Yeah, you were acting like me," Jamie laughed and rolled his eyes at Travis as though he were being too serious.

"Jamie," Autumn said, turning toward him and placing her two hands on his shoulders so he couldn't get away.

153

"When I was spiraling you knew just what to say to me. When you heard the text messages from Noah you knew he was going to hurt himself. Visiting Donna and talking with her, you knew how to comfort her. How can someone who says so much dumb shit, be so intuitive and empathetic."

"Practice," he admitted, immediately staring down at his shoes. "My mother, she's got crap wrong with her mind. I grew up trying to get her to keep her shit together and not get in trouble."

"She's alive?" Autumn asked, crouching a bit, trying to pull his eyes back up toward her. "I just assumed that she was the person you went to grief counseling for."

"She's alive," he shot back curtly. "But she's nuts. And I got good at spotting crazy and trying to make it better."

Travis touched Autumn's arm gently and broke the moment. "You should get checked out too. Do you want us to give you a lift to the hospital?"

"I don't need to," Autumn said, waving him off. She was mad at first that he'd interrupted what Jamie might have just shared with her, but the more she thought about it, Travis seemed to do most things with a good reason.

"We'd offer to take you for a bite to eat, but you look like a freaking mental patient in your ripped up pajamas," Jamie teased, and just like that he was back to his old self.

"I just want to go home." Autumn sighed, looking at the two men and thinking of them the way Noah had just said. Umbrellas, shelter from the worst the storm could give you. "But we can order pizza or something."

"That sounds good." Travis smiled. "I let you drive here Jamie, but there is no way in hell you're driving us back to Autumn's house. You're a maniac."

"I'll drive." Autumn plucked the keys from Jamie's hand. "Jamie, you can take my car back for me."

"No way," Jamie argued, but it was too late. Autumn tossed him her keys and slid into the driver's seat of his sports car.

"Really?" Travis asked as he sat in the passenger seat and buckled up.

"I couldn't care less about driving this thing, but for the look on his face right now, it's totally worth it."

"You're amazing." Travis sighed. "What you did today, coming here and risking your life. What did you say to him to get him to change his mind?"

"I don't know," Autumn admitted. "I honestly don't feel like it was me talking. Charlie was so good in those high-stress moments. I tried to think what he would do."

"I'm sure he's proud," Travis assured her with a large smile.

"I think he would be," Autumn replied. "I never thought I could help someone when I feel so helpless myself. It makes me kind of hopeful; maybe I can get through this."

"I'm sorry that I stopped you when you were talking to Jamie," Travis apologized, biting nervously at his lip. "He's going to tell you someday where all his crap comes from. I can tell he is, but it's not going to be because you ask him a thousand questions. In fact every one you ask makes him clam up even more. I just wanted to stop you from pushing him, so you'd get your chance to hear it from him someday."

"Thank you. Jamie is so much more than I gave him credit for when I met him. I can see why you aren't willing to give up on him."

"I know it looks like I'm helping him, but there've been plenty of days he hasn't given up on me even when I don't deserve to have him stick around."

"I guess we jerks better stick together." Autumn sighed, as she thought how much her life had changed in the last few months.

"Probably, since no one else will put up with us."

Chapter Thirty-Two

Noah's refusal to open his eyes didn't keep him from knowing exactly where he was. He'd never done the math, but he could assume as much of his life was spent in the hospital as it had been spent out. That meant he could recognize the smell of the industrial cleaners and the sound of a blood pressure machine. The squeeze of the cuff on his arm as it filled with air made it all more real than he wanted it to be.

He heard the door squeak open and wondered which doctor or nurse he'd spent the last ten years working with was about to come in. To have his peers treating him like a patient was his worst nightmare.

He split his eyes open and readied himself for a fight. Even with everything that had happened, he still had rage brewing in him.

"Noah," a familiar voice whispered from behind a large vase of flowers.

"Donna?" he croaked out.

"Yes, I wasn't sure if you'd be awake. I hope it's all right I stopped by. There was just something I wanted to share with you." She placed the vase on the small sill of the window, and he finally looked around the room.

"What hospital is this?" he asked, realizing the wallpaper was a slightly different putrid yellow than the hospital he worked in.

"The EMTs decided you might be more comfortable here at East General, and it wasn't that much farther. It would be more private for you." She didn't sit in the chair next to his bed or make a move to slip out of her coat. Donna didn't look like she planned to stay.

"That was thoughtful," Noah said, truly grateful for the gift of privacy. "Thank you for the flowers."

"Sure," Donna said with a tired smile. "It's the least I can do. I really want to apologize if I made you feel like your life wasn't worth living. The police had me go by your house, and I read the note you left. My intention was never to put so much pressure on you."

"What did you want?" Noah asked, genuinely curious about what would bring Donna peace.

He was surprised when she pushed out an exhausted chuckle. "I'm not sure," she admitted. "I wanted you to be in pain. Or at least to show it the same way I was. It was selfish and insensitive of me."

"You're neither of those things, Donna. You tried many times, and I just kept pushing you away. I'm not just talking about after the accident. I was always trying to keep my distance from you." Noah closed his eyes and rested his head back onto the stiff pillow.

"When I got to your place, Noah, I saw the journal you were reading. The page was folded over and I saw the entry about Paris. I have to admit something, and I want you to know it's very hard for me. For quite a while Rayanne and I argued about her relationship with you. I felt like she was giving up so much just to be with you."

"So we have more in common than we thought," Noah cut in, but she stepped forward quickly and waved him off.

"No," she asserted. "It's only because I didn't understand. One of the last times we fought about it, I brought up Paris. This was years ago. You hadn't shown up for some family picnic, and I was aggravated with you. I asked Rayanne why she kept sacrificing everything she loved for a man who couldn't even show up when she needed him."

"Maybe it would have been better if she had listened to you." Noah sighed, thinking of all the events he missed.

"She never for a minute agreed with me," Donna insisted. "As a matter of fact, she looked me dead in the eyes and told me you were her Paris. No part of the world, no famous landmark or old café would ever compare to how you made her feel. It's one of the last times I ever bothered to have that argument again. My daughter had a mind of her own, and if she didn't want to be with you, she would have left. You made her happier than those things she walked away from."

"I don't know," Noah shrugged, finally opening his eyes again. "Maybe you're right. I just wish I'd have given her more of a voice. That's what changed my mind in all of this."

"I heard Autumn was there on the side of the road with you."

"She asked me if I were giving Rayanne a choice in all this, what would she choose? I couldn't take anything else away from her. She'd want me to live." Noah wiped at a tear and cleared his throat for composure.

"I have something else for you." Donna reached into her pocket and pulled out a small box. "Autumn asked me to give this to you." She put the box in his hand and waited for him to open it.

As he lifted the lid he let out a small laugh. Pulling it out by the key chain loop, he looked down at the silver umbrella. It spun as he dangled it in front of his face.

"Does it mean something to you?" Donna asked, scrutinizing the trinket.

"It just means I'm not alone," he said, looking over at Donna and reaching his hand out. She looked afraid to take it, but almost more scared not to. As though the chance might disappear and never present itself again.

<u>Chapter Thirty-Three</u>

Five Months Later

"I don't get it; why does Jamie have a gift for us? We're supposed to be celebrating him. It's his birthday, and he's finally off probation." Autumn stood on tiptoes to look at the note in Travis's hand.

"He said it's in his room." Travis led Autumn down the hallway. "I can only imagine what it is."

"Maybe he cleaned his room." She laughed as though that were completely ridiculous. When Travis threw the door open her giggle stopped, and she gasped. "Or cleaned it out."

"Oh kid," Travis said, stepping into the bedroom that was now all bare walls and empty opened dresser drawers.

"Where is he? Do you think he got his own place?" Autumn asked, trying to salvage the hope that was dwindling away.

"No," Travis said solemnly. He reached down to the stripped bare mattress and grabbed the paper that was folded in half and read it aloud.

Trav,

You and Autumn can say all you want that you aren't dating. I get it. It's too soon and you're waiting for the right time. I don't think that time is too far off, and I don't want to be in the way. I think you guys actually have a great shot at being happy. For a tight-ass like you, that's something that might not come around again. You know as well as I do at some point I'll screw it up for you. After all you've done for me, I don't think I could deal with that.

Have a little faith,
Jamie

Travis let out a tired laugh, and all Autumn could do was rub her hand over his sagged shoulders.

"We need to go after him," she asserted, not wanting to be the thing standing in the way of them working this out. Jamie hadn't really been a burden over the last few months, but he hadn't completely changed his ways either, and she didn't want to see him go. He was her friend, and a real one was hard to come by.

"No, that's not what he wants. I just have to let him go." Travis lowered the note to his side and looked around the empty room.

"What happens when he gets in trouble and you aren't there to bail him out? He needs you." Autumn felt her nerves going haywire, considering all the problems Jamie might have out in the world by himself. "How much money could he possibly have? He won't get very far."

"Jamie has some unique skills that quickly make him money," Travis explained.

"Those same skills get him in a hell of a lot of trouble, don't they?" she asked, cocking an eyebrow at him.

"Have a little faith," Travis smiled. "I used to say that to him all the time when he first came to live with me, and it would make him so mad. He's right too; it was a cop-out. It's what I would say when I didn't have an answer. But over time when I'd tell him to have a little faith he'd just nod. Eventually I feel like he started to actually believe me. But I've never heard him say it before."

"He's been listening to you all these years, Travis," Autumn assured him. "I'm just sorry to see him go. I hope he really doesn't think he needed to leave for our sake. He's not going to ruin anything."

"Jamie thinks everything he touches falls apart. He doesn't believe he can actually be a part of something without poisoning it. I've never been able to convince him that wasn't true."

Autumn nodded her head, understanding perfectly what it was like to fear your effect on other people. Was sadness as toxic as radiation? "Mike is back in town for the week before he heads out for treatment in Boston. I was looking forward to him meeting both of you over the weekend." She slumped her shoulders in disappointment. She was sure Mike would really like a kid like Jamie. "And dinner tonight," she said, remembering their plans for the three of them to grab a bite to eat at the Italian place.

"He's got an answer for that too," Travis smiled, flipping the note over. "Jamie made reservations for two at Chez-Jean tonight at seven."

"Are you kidding me? That place is impossible to get into. The wait list is usually a couple months long. How in the world would he have gotten that reservation?"

"He's relentless," Travis said. He wasn't just talking about how Jamie had gotten the nearly impossible reservation, but that he was pretty much forcing their first date. "We don't have to go if you don't want to. I'm fine if we just grab some takeout."

Autumn pondered the idea of a night out with Travis. Jamie had been right. They were taking their time. And a foolproof way to not get too close was to always have Jamie around. With him gone, they'd have to take a good hard look at what they were doing. "I don't know." She shrugged. "I haven't been dressed up in so long, maybe it wouldn't be so bad."

"That's a ringing endorsement." Travis laughed. "Dinner with me might not be that bad. I should put that on a bumper sticker."

"You know what I mean," she said, jabbing her elbow into his ribs. "Last chance though, you sure you don't want to go after Jamie? I'm with you if you want to."

"It makes me happy to know you care about him. Being the only one can get exhausting. I'm going to give him his space for now. If he needs me I hope he calls."

"Do you think he will?" Autumn asked, looking around the empty room, already feeling a pang of sadness over Jamie's absence.

"If you asked me six months ago I'd have said no. Jamie's convinced himself that he's better off on his own. He believes he can fix his problems, and the only reason I was ever there was because I forced my way into his life."

"He told me one night," Autumn said quietly. "I know about what happened to him. We didn't talk much about it. He didn't seem like he wanted to go into details. I can understand why he doesn't ask for help. I give you a lot of credit for never giving up on him."

"I always knew if I gave up on him, that would be it for him. I was the last line of defense between him and . . ." he trailed off not really sure what would be the fate of someone like Jamie if they were left alone.

"Have a little faith," Autumn said, rubbing her hand over his back again.

He nodded and pulled her into a hug. "I'm glad Jamie found you and in some weird way brought us together."

"I don't know what my life is supposed to be like anymore, Travis. I'd already had it all planned out, and now everything is different." She felt his chin rest on the top of her head as he hugged her a little tighter. "Now the only thing I can do is make sure today makes sense. So let's go get dressed up and have a fancy dinner, just the two of us."

"I'm never going to pressure you, Autumn," Travis promised.

"I know." She smiled, pulling away and looking up at his serious face. "And if it makes you feel better about Jamie, I can break into a store on the way to the restaurant and steal some stuff. If you're looking for a new cause, I can stir up lots of trouble."

"I think I'll just appreciate the peace and quiet, but thanks." Travis looked around the empty room one more time as Autumn took his hand and led him out.

"One day at a time," she whispered as she closed the bedroom door and laced her fingers with his. "The storm isn't over, but at least every now and then we can see the sun. Even if it's just long enough to remind us it's still there." She lost her breath for a moment as his arm wrapped around her shoulder. It reminded her what it felt like to belong to someone.

"I don't mind the rain," Travis said quietly, "as long as I'm in good company."

The End

Continue the story in the Rough Waters Series in *The Runaway Storm*.

Books by Danielle Stewart

Piper Anderson Series:
Book 1: Chasing Justice
Book 2: Cutting Ties
Book 3: Changing Fate
Book 4: Finding Freedom
Book 5: Settling Scores
Book 6: Battling Destiny
Book 7: Chris & Sydney Collection – Choosing
Christmas & Saving Love
Betty's Journal - Bonus Material (suggested to be read
after Book 4 to avoid spoilers)

Edenville Series – A Piper Anderson Spin Off:
Book 1: Flowers in the Snow
Book 2: Kiss in the Wind
Book 3: Stars in a Bottle

The Clover Series:
Hearts of Clover - Novella & Book 2: (Half My Heart &
Change My Heart)
Book 3: All My Heart
Book 4: Facing Home

Rough Waters Series:
Book 1: The Goodbye Storm
Book 2: The Runaway Storm

Midnight Magic Series:
Amelia

Author Information

One random newsletter subscriber will be chosen every month this year. The chosen subscriber will receive a $25 eGift Card! Sign up today by visiting www.authordaniellestewart.com

Author Contact:
Website: AuthorDanielleStewart.com
Email: AuthorDanielleStewart@Gmail.com
Facebook: Author Danielle Stewart
Twitter: @DStewartAuthor

33557570R00103

Made in the USA
Middletown, DE
18 July 2016